Final Takedown

Also by Brent R. Sherrard
In the SideStreets series:
Wasted

Final Takedown

Brent R. Sherrard

James Lorimer & Company Ltd., Publishers
Toronto

James Lorimer & Company Ltd., Publishers acknowledges the support of the Ontario Arts Council. We acknowledge the financial support of the Government of Canada through the Canada Book Fund for our publishing activities. We acknowledge the support of the Canada Council for the Arts for our publishing program. We acknowledge the Government of Ontario through the Ontario Media Development Corporation's Ontario Book Initiative.

Cover design: Meredith Bangay   Cover image: iStock

Library and Archives Canada Cataloguing in Publication

Sherrard, Brent R.
        Final takedown / Brent R. Sherrard.
Issued also in an electronic format.

ISBN 978-1-55277-523-3 (pbk.).—ISBN 978-1-55277-525-7 (bound)
I. Title.

PS8637.H488F56 2010   jC813'.6   C2010-902621-7

James Lorimer &
Company Ltd., Publishers
317 Adelaide Street West,
Suite 1002
Toronto, ON
M5V 1P9
www.lorimer.ca

Distributed in the United
States by:
Orca Book Publishers
P.O. Box 468
Custer, WA USA
98240-0468

Printed and bound in Canada.
Manufactured by Printcrafters in Winnipeg, Manitoba, Canada in August 2010.
Job # 27288

For my mother, Phoebe.
Thanks for taking the time to read to me, Ma.

Chapter 1

"Elias Heath Minto and Jordan Peter Black, you will reappear before this court on . . ." The judge pauses. He casts a bored look over his bifocals at the court clerk, who is rifling frantically through a huge black ledger. After a few uncomfortable minutes the clerk heaves a sigh and tells the judge, "June 17, Your Honour. Nine a.m."

"You will reappear before this court on June 17 at nine a.m.," the judge repeats. "That gives you seven weeks. In the meantime, I suggest you both find good lawyers, and if you value your freedom at all, my advice is that you walk the straight and narrow, gentlemen. The clerk will prepare an undertaking, which you will sign before leaving these premises. Dismissed."

I look at Jordan, who shrugs his shoulders and starts to walk away. I fall in behind him, heading for the back of the gallery, and freedom. After spending the night in a chilly holding cell at the police station, I can't wait to step outside into the warm May sunshine.

We pass the court-appointed lawyer who'd stood up for us. She seems totally bored with the whole process. Jordan ignores her, but seeing as we have no money to hire an attorney, chances are she'll be representing us again in seven weeks. It seems like a smart idea to stay on her good side.

"Miss Trevors?" I say.

"Yes?" she replies without looking up.

"I just wanted to say thank you," I tell her.

"You're welcome." She seems a little upset, maybe the remark from the judge about us getting a *good* lawyer pissed her off.

"Your papers will be ready in about an hour, front desk," the clerk says over his shoulder as he breezes by. I catch up to Jordan on the front steps, where he's lighting a cigarette. He passes it to me. I take a long drag as I lean against the courthouse wall.

"Let's go," he says.

"We have to wait. We need to sign those papers," I tell him. He let outs a huge sigh of disgust, like it's my fault. I'm just glad we're allowed to leave at all.

"You boys are lucky you got Cameron," a voice announces from behind us. We spin around to see the cop who arrested us yesterday. He's giving us his best power-stare. Jordan laughs.

"You think this is funny?"

"No, I think *you're* funny," Jordan tells him.

"We'll see how funny you find the lock-up."

"Self-defence, man. You got to be able to defend yourself," Jordan says to him.

"Minto," the cop says, shifting his attention to me. "Not many Mintos around here. Any chance I know your father?"

"If you do, that'd make one of us," I tell him. I barely remember what my father looks like. My clearest memory of him is watching his white pickup truck drive away, and my mom dragging me into the house as I screamed for him not to go. I was four at the time. I haven't seen or heard from him since.

"Heath Minto," he remembers, snapping his fingers. "Real hard-ass, or at least thought he was. I heard he ended up in the pen out West somewhere."

"I hope he's still there," I mutter. If he'd known my father, it should've been easier to recognize me by face than by name. My father's father was from Malaysia. He'd met my grandmother, a full-blooded Maliseet, while the freighter he'd worked on was docked at the local wharf. They'd formed a relationship over the three weeks his ship had been hauled up for repairs and, without knowing it, he'd left an unborn son behind when he'd sailed. I'm dark-skinned. My brown eyes have a noticeable slant to them, just like my father's, according to Mom. Jordan calls me a *Chindian* — as in half-Chinese, half-Indian.

The hour ticks by slowly before we can go inside to sign the undertaking. Jordan scribbles his name and hustles away, not even bothering to read it. Basically, it says we're to stay away from alcohol and drugs, and to keep out of trouble. If we breach the conditions, we'll be thrown into juvie until our court appearance. I sign it and leave.

"All right, let's get out of here," Jordan says. We've barely cleared the courthouse property when he pulls a joint from behind his ear and starts to light it. The cops checked everywhere but there. That's exactly the kind of thing that proves to Jordan that he's smarter than everybody else.

I take a quick look back to make sure no cops are behind us, and there's Jordan's mom, pulling up next to us in her old red beater. Jordan sees her and slips the joint into his jacket pocket.

"Get in," she orders.

"And good morning to *you*," Jordan answers as we climb in.

"Don't get smart with me, Jordan," she almost yells. "What the hell is this, anyway?"

"Aw, it's no big deal, just a scam —" he starts to say, but she cuts him off.

"Just a scam? Are you out of your mind? Aggravated assault and uttering death threats is certainly no *small* deal," she says. "If Tanya hadn't called me this morning, I still wouldn't know you'd been arrested. Why didn't you call last night?"

"I didn't want to bother you, so I called her instead," Jordan says.

We drive in silence. I stare out the window at the filthy streets of Helmsdale. It seems like every fourth house has a "for sale" sign in the yard. Like a lot of small East Coast towns, it has always relied on natural resources for its prosperity. Now the pulp mill is gone, along with the potash mine. Anybody with any sense is bailing out, heading for the big cities or out West for the oil boom.

Mrs. Black pulls into the parking lot of the call-centre where she works, saying that she doesn't have time to drive us home. She has to get back to the phones.

"You'll probably want to stay with us for a few days, Elias," she says.

"Yeah, okay," I tell her. The welfare cheques just came in, so Mom'll be drunk now until she runs low on money. I'll sneak over later and steal enough from her for the rent and groceries. It's the same thing every month.

We walk to Jordan's place, smoking the joint along the way. As soon as we get there, he heads for the shower. I sit on the deck, thinking about how this all started, the afternoon before.

Chapter 2

Jordan and I were heading out to the bus compound behind the school to smoke a joint before English class. As we crossed the parking lot, we had to walk by Cody Morgan and a handful of his buddies. They were admiring Cody's brand-new pickup truck. Cody was the captain of the hockey team, a big guy with a big mouth. His folks were well off.

As we passed by, Cody was bragging about how much the truck cost. Jordan and Cody's eyes met, just for a moment, but Jordan thought he'd been given "the look." The one that said, "I'm better than you. You're trash. I've got a new truck; you've got nothing." It didn't matter whether he'd imagined it or not, Jordan wasn't about to take any chances.

"Hey, Cody," he said. "Any asshole can drive a new truck."

"Oh yeah, then why don't you?" Cody replied.

"Because I'm not any asshole," Jordan said.

Now Cody had to save face, so he asked Jordan how he'd like a punch in the mouth.

"Love one," Jordan said, calling his bluff.

"Yeah, all right then, tough guy. Why don't we settle this right now?"

"No time like the present, sweetheart," Jordan replied.

A casual observer might have thought we were heading into the lion's den, but Jordan and me were no strangers to bare-knuckle brawls, or being outnumbered. We'd been swapping punches with anyone who wanted to go since we were in grade school, so we both knew exactly how it would go down. Cody would run his mouth, going for the bluff, seeing as he had plenty of back-up. Or so he thought.

Jordan would force Cody to move first, as usual. Then he'd flatten him. Not many people ever stood up to a shot from Jordan — or for that matter, from me either. If anyone tried to step in, I'd drop them.

My heart was hammering, and I had to force myself to breathe deeply. Some people might call that fear. But I know by now it's just the flight-or-fight response — and I'm no runner.

"Think there's enough of you?" Jordan asked with a smirk.

"One is more than enough," Cody said, stepping away from the group. He rolled his shoulders like a boxer warming up. His buddies smirked at us.

They were all big guys. Bigger than us, anyway. If your family has enough money to keep you in hockey season after season, they can probably afford to feed you well, too. Every one of these guys was built like the weightlifters they were, while we were slim and hard. We'd got that way from shovelling, swinging axes at blocks of firewood, and ripping punches into the sand-filled duffle bag Jordan had hanging in his basement.

Cody's number-two man identified himself by moving slightly away from the group, and I smiled at him. It was Tommy Mansfred, whose dad owns the local hardware store. For just a fraction of a second I saw fear flash across his face. He tried to hide it with a sneer, but it was too late. I smiled harder.

"I'm sure you guys want to get back to making out, so let's get this done," Jordan said, stepping within striking range of Cody. His hands were down, and he looked like he was willing to take a punch in the face and call it quits. Cody stepped up and slammed both palms into his shoulders, which caused Jordan to rock back a step. Bad move.

Jordan smiled and said, "That all you've got, *asshole*?"

Cody made his move, the exact one Jordan had known he would make.

These guys weren't street fighters, they were hockey fighters. Cody grabbed Jordan's sweater in his left hand, just below the neck, and threw his right fist toward Jordan's face. His plan would be to fire as many as he could before the referee or linesman broke it up. Every hockey fight was the same.

But this was no hockey fight. Before the punch had travelled halfway to its target, Jordan caught it in the palm of his left hand, casually deflecting it over his shoulder. Cody had his mouth open and his head tipped back as he reloaded, but it was already too late.

With his chin in the air, Cody ate a vicious right hook. He never saw it coming. It was short and tight and right on the money, and when it hit his chin it sounded like a rock bouncing off a brick wall. Just like that, Cody was on the ground. He wasn't about to get up anytime soon.

I almost missed my cue as Tommy, showing more guts than brains, made a charge for Jordan. I stepped to my left and met him coming in with a straight left hand. He was big and tough, but bloodied as he staggered backwards clutching his eye. I'd split his eyebrow wide open. The blood pouring down his face took all the fight out of him.

So it was over, just as we'd expected. With their leader down, and his backup bleeding like a stuck pig, the other three guys just stood there. I figured if I was them, I'd do the same thing.

"Ladies?" I said, but got no takers.

"Let's go have that toke," Jordan said. I looked back as we walked away and saw blood splattered all over the fender of Cody's new truck.

I couldn't help thinking how cool we were, two guys most people wouldn't give a second glance, and we'd just basically destroyed the school's athletic heroes. It was a nice feeling, knowing that those guys would spend the rest of their lives trying to forget that it wasn't money and popularity that really mattered. What really mattered was heart.

***

Ten minutes later we were sitting in class, stoned again, pretending to listen to Mr. Tarver.

"When you start to think that you are smart, *that* is the beginning of stupidity," Tarver said as he scrawled it on the board in blue chalk. "Think about that, people. I'll be back in a few minutes."

We watched Tarver as he left the classroom, twenty-two bored — but, at least for the moment, amused — Grade 11 students. Watching Mr. Tarver walk out was the highlight of his English class.

First, there was the way he dressed. Polyester pants that stopped way short of his shoes, which always looked like they'd been used to scrape something nasty from a sidewalk. His pants were always tucked firmly between his butt cheeks, as if on purpose. I could picture him getting ready to leave the house in the morning, then stopping to insert as much material as he could into his crack, maybe with a spatula.

I busted out laughing at the picture in my mind. Jordan and I had no illusions about being smart, at least not in the way Mr. Tarver meant. I still couldn't identify the all-important parts of a sentence, for instance. But when it came to real smarts, the kind you needed to survive in the street, we were honour students.

"Care to share the joke with the class?" Mr. Tarver said as he spun at the door.

"Nah," I replied.

He shook his head, causing the permanent cowlick that stuck up proudly from the crown of his head to sway back and forth like a sunburned sheaf of wheat in a soft summer breeze. I decided to go for it, seeing how proud he'd be of my descriptive ability.

"When you shake your head like that, your cowlick reminds me of a sunburned sheaf of wheat bobbing gently on a soft summer breeze," I said.

"Excellent!" he exclaimed. "Poetic and concise, a truly splendid verbal portrait. I commend you, Eli. Class?"

"I think it was beautiful," said The Chest, widening her eyes and trying to look smart.

The Chest's real name is Tina Bradley. She's as dumb as a stump, but built like a lingerie model. She usually only dates older guys with fancy cars, but for some reason she seems to have a thing for Jordan. I've seen her stealing glances at him, but he seems not to notice. I wish she'd check me out.

"I shall return," said Mr. Tarver as Tina tried to tear the buttons loose from her blouse by hauling her shoulders back and thrusting her breasts forward. Someday, I thought, someone's going to lose an eye.

The best part of watching Mr. Tarver walk was

the walk itself. His heels never touched the floor, except when he was standing still, and each time one of his feet touched down, he'd slide it ahead a bit, causing a scraping sound. It looked like he was walking on really thin ice, testing each step and hoping he didn't go through. The clothes, the world-class wedgie, the haircut that looked like he did it himself with a hatchet and a mirror, and the strange walk made him look like a character from a comedy sketch disappearing from view.

I looked around the class, wondering if anyone else was thinking about Tarver's latest attempt to prod us into using our heads. He was always dropping little bombs like that on us, hoping that we might learn to think deeper and further than what the next few hours might bring. I could have told him he was wasting his time.

More than half the class came from broken homes, for starters. There were four of us who'd been raised by our mothers alone since before we'd started school. We were all poor, and not what you'd call motivated. I wondered what Mr. Tarver and others like him expected from students who took Level Three courses anyway. We were either too stupid to handle anything harder, or we just didn't care one way or the other.

Jordan and me were taking vocational, or what was commonly called Shop. Carpentry, to be specific. We figured it was practical, a lot cleaner than motor mechanics, and much less dangerous than electrical. We thought that, if we could get some money together, after we finished school we could start buying old houses cheap and fixing them up, turning them over for big profits — if the economy ever improved. My stomach flopped when I thought of the scheme that Jordan had hinted about a few days before. He said it would be risky but, if it worked, we'd be set, and maybe more.

The class heard the distinctive "*schiff, schiff*" of Mr. Tarver's leather-soled shoes scuffing the floor long before he came into view. By the time he'd entered the classroom I could picture him thinking what great students we'd become, everyone sitting quietly at attention. Maybe he was even foolish enough to think we'd been pondering the meaning of his cryptic quote. If so, he quickly found out he was wrong.

The first three kids he asked all claimed they had no idea what it might've meant. That was the easy way out. The fourth person he asked was Jordan, who never takes the easy way out.

"Jordan, would you care to try?" Mr. Tarver asked.

"Well, the way I see it is, if you think you're smart, you'll quit trying to learn, or something like that. If you quit learning, you won't get any smarter, that's for sure."

"Excellent, Jordan. Well put! When you start to think you're smart, or I should say, start to think you're *too* smart, you become afraid to ask questions. You don't want to look like you don't know, you don't want to look stupid. No one knows everything. We all learn every day, or at least we should. So, by not asking questions, trying not to look stupid, you end up doing just that. That, my friends, is stupidity. *Not* knowing isn't stupid; *choosing* not to know is stupid."

I liked Jordan's answer better. He'd said the same thing, and it hadn't hurt my head.

We spent the rest of the class discussing the imagery contained in classical poetry. That was the thing about school I could never understand. Most of what we were supposed to learn had no practical value at all. I pictured Jordan and me renovating a house, replacing a rotted-out floor sill, and having a difficult time with it.

"What do you think, should we brace the wall up further, or jackhammer some of the foundation wall out and replace it later?" I'd ask.

"I don't know, but that Yeats could sure paint a verbal picture of epic magnitude, could he not?"

I snickered out loud, attempting to turn it into a cough, but Mr. Tarver wasn't fooled.

"What is it now, Elias? My hair again?"

"No sir," I replied.

"Are you ready for Thursday?" he asked.

"I will be," I told him. Both Jordan and I would be ready, because we'd be wearing our "smart" shoes.

Jordan wasn't just smart, he was brilliant. He'd discovered that you could write stuff on the soles of your shoes with a pencil, and then erase it instantly by giving your foot a firm scuff on the floor. We'd just go into class early, take seats beside each other, and copy all of the difficult stuff onto our soles. By casually crossing our legs, we could read our own notes, and each others'. The teachers were so intent on watching for cellphones and stuff that our low-tech system slipped right by.

There was a loud knock, and Tarver rushed to the classroom door. Kids were always knocking while class was in session, and then running. But this time it was no prank. It was Mr. Boyd, the principal. My heart froze when I saw the two cops standing behind him.

Chapter 3

So here I am, sitting in the warm sun on Jordan's deck. I'm happy for the time being not to be sitting in a jail cell.

"Feel like another joint?" Jordan asks, stepping outside.

"Sure, why not," I say. I figure if I get high enough I'll lose that sinking feeling I can't seem to shake.

It doesn't work. By the time the joint is finished, I'm officially paranoid. I can't stop thinking about going to jail and getting raped. I know that, if that ever happens, I'll kill someone, and then I'll never get out. That one punch will have ended my life. From high-school student to prison lifer in one shot.

We go inside and Jordan puts on a CD. A friend burned it for him — fourteen heavy-metal rock songs he likes to play full blast. I'm not in the mood, so I tell him I'm heading to my place, but I won't be long.

As I walk, I'm starting to come down, and I begin to think about how the only thing that I've ever taken pride in has been the fact that I'm tough. Now we're probably heading for juvie because of it. Why couldn't Jordan have just ignored Cody? Why couldn't he have just walked away? I know why. He's the same as me — being tough is how we define ourselves.

At home, Mom is sitting at the kitchen table, a bottle of vodka in front of her. She always starts out by mixing fancy little drinks, trying to add some class to her binge, but that doesn't last long. By the second day, she's drinking straight from the bottle, all pretence of social drinking lost.

"Why aren't you in school?" she slurs. "I have no privacy. I need my privacy."

I ignore her and look for her purse, which I find in the bathroom. I take out enough money for the rent and groceries, then tuck fifty bucks away in my room. I'll give it to her later in the month, and she'll think I'm a great guy.

Every month since I can remember, Mom gets drunk for a week when the welfare comes. The rest of the time she works in the kitchen at Burke's Diner, peeling vegetables and washing dishes during the supper rush. They pay her in cash, so it won't affect her welfare, but they know better than to call her when she's on her monthly spree. I guess they feel sorry for her.

As I come back into the kitchen, I feel a surge of anger as I look at her. Is her drinking the reason why my father ran off? Had she always gone on a binge at the start of the month, or was it just since my father left?

"When did Heath leave?" I ask as I return to the kitchen.

"A long time ago," she mumbles.

"No, I mean what was the date, what time of the month?"

"October the thirtieth. I took you out trick-or-treating that year, all by myself. You never even said thank you, and now my privacy means nothing," she says, taking a slug of vodka. "You're just like him, always here when you shouldn't be, and never here when you should be."

As the screen door slams shut behind me, I think about how I hope that makes sense to her, because it doesn't to me.

I walk to the grocery store, stopping at the landlord's place first to drop off the rent money. He gives me a receipt, and I ask him when he plans on fixing the roof. Every time it rains, I have my own private waterfall in my bedroom. But every time I ask, I get the same answer: "Fix it yerself," he says. "Ya get the place cheap enough, consider yerself lucky."

At the grocery store I buy all the specials I can find. Then I decide to splurge and pick up a huge steak. When the cashier rings up my order, I'm four bucks short, and really embarrassed.

"You'll have to put something back," she says.

"The steak," I say. The fact that one steak is out

24

of my league really pisses me off.

The store is nearly empty, and as I walk down the meat aisle I make a decision. I casually slip the steak down the front of my pullover, tucking it down into my pants, and zip my jacket up half way.

"Sorry about that," I tell the girl as I return. I hastily pay and gather up my grocery bags and put them back into the cart. When I'm nearly through the sliding glass doors of the supermarket, I hear her call out, "Hey, you forget somethin'?"

Busted, I think. I have a split second to decide whether to bolt or bluff my way out of it. There's a family blocking my way to the street. I'll have to bluff.

"Like what?" I say, turning back to the girl. "I didn't have enough money for what I had."

She holds up a package of toilet paper and waves it at me. "Then you better come back and get this, or you'll be in trouble later."

I get the toilet paper and wheel my cart out into the parking lot. I realize as I gather the bags into my hands that I'll never make it to my place without losing something. I put everything back into the cart and start for home.

I just clear the parking lot when a siren sounds right behind me, just a quick blurp, like a lovesick moose. I nearly jump clear of my shoes. The steak slips out and plops on the sidewalk as I turn to see a cop car pull up behind me. The same two cops who'd arrested me the day before get out.

"You stealing that?" one of them asks.

So, the cashier saw after all. What a stupid move, I think. Now they'll lock me up until my court date, all because I thought I deserved a steak.

"You deaf? I asked you if you were stealing that cart," he says.

"No, I had too much stuff to carry. I was going to bring it back," I tell him. The steak still lies accusingly on the pavement.

"They can't leave store property. That's theft," his partner, a female cop, says. "We'll give you a break. Take it back." She points to the ground. "You dropped something there."

I throw the steak into the cart, and trudge back to the store. Gathering up the bags again, I start to walk away. It's going to be a long trek. I've just gotten back out to the street when the cruiser drives by me again, really slow, with both cops looking right at me. This time I'm sure they're going to bust me, but it's just the paranoia of coming down off the weed.

I make it home and put the groceries away. Mom is passed out on the couch, so I take the half-full bottle of vodka from the table and fill it up to three-quarters with water. I grab the steak and head back to Jordan's place.

He's lying on the deck with his eyes closed when I get there. Music is blasting through an open window. Jordan opens his eyes when he notices me walking on the deck. I can tell by the look of him that he's smoked another joint. It seems like lately all we do is get high.

"Let's fry this up," I say, showing him the steak.

"Okay, but first, let's fry ourselves," he says. I'm really hungry, but I help him smoke the joint anyway. I'm relieved when it does the trick. It's no fun when I get paranoid, but after the day I've had, the comfortable numbness is just what I need.

We're sitting on the step, lost in our own thoughts, when Jordan starts to laugh. He's always coming up with crazy ideas when he's high. I wait until he gets a grip on himself before I ask what's up.

"The plan," he says. "You know, the takedown. It's the one that's going to set us up. It's brilliant, I'm telling you. Two minutes and we'll be rolling in it."

I don't know much about this new scheme of his. All he's told me so far is that there's a lot of money involved for little work. In the last year, Jordan has come up with two takedowns, both of which we've successfully pulled off. First, there was this guy at school, Jerry Dickson, who sold joints for five bucks a pop. Jordan found out he was actually dealing for an older guy who gave him a joint for every five he sold. Jordan figured Jerry was selling maybe fifteen or twenty a day, so by the end of the week, he'd have four or five hundred dollars on him. Jordan had scoped the whole thing out before he'd sprung it on me. When Jerry left home to go to his dealer's on Friday night to drop off the week's take and collect his stash for the following one, we took him down. We scored two hundred and sixty-five bucks each for our troubles. Then, a few months later, we broke into a bootlegger's house while he made his usual Friday-morning trip to the liquor store to stock up for the weekend. Jordan had been sure there'd be thousands of dollars stashed somewhere in the house. We ended up with eight hundred bucks that we found in a coffee can on the kitchen table, and a bad scare when we heard footsteps coming from the back of the house. I barely had time to yell "Go!" before I hightailed it out the door and into the woods. Jordan had to dive out an upstairs window, then jump off the porch roof. He twisted his ankle. As he limped toward the bushes where I stood watching, Arlo Dunphy, an old booze-pig, came out onto the back step with a rifle in his hands. He fired a shot into the air and yelled for Jordan to stop, which of course made him forget his ankle and take off like a scalded cat. I nearly shit my pants. Jordan still laughs about it, but it showed me just how quickly things could go wrong.

"So, what is it this time?" I ask, hoping it's not something stupid that could get us killed, or sent away for a long time, like an armed robbery.

"Okay," he says. "I've scoped this out myself. I stumbled onto it one morning sneaking back from Tanya's place, so what I tell you is for sure. You know Jack Hargrove, right?"

"Yeah," I reply. Jack is the closest thing we have to a real gangster in Helmsdale.

"Okay, he's got illegal video gambling machines set up around town. Pretty near everyone knows that, right? He's not getting busted, so for sure someone is greasing someone's palm. Well, every Sunday morning Jack drives over to Bateman's Motel, and parks around the back. Since they renovated the front part of the building, those rooms aren't being used, *except* for room number six. He gets out and knocks on the door, and this real nervous-looking old guy answers. Jack hands him a bag, then gets in his car and leaves. The old guy drives away about a half-hour later. He's alone. I watched him leave two weeks in a row. You with me so far?"

"Not really," I say.

Jordan sighs. "It's obvious Jack's giving a cut of the money from the machines to him. The old guy is a bag man! His car's got Quebec licence plates, so he must be part of some big operation, probably collects all over the place. I figure there's probably ten thousand bucks or more, just from Helmsdale alone. Who knows, the old boy might have a hundred thousand on him. What do you think about that?"

"Good for him," I say. "How are we supposed to get it?"

"That's where The Chest comes in."

"Tina Bradley?" I ask. "What's she got to do with us?"

"She's getting a thousand bucks to do what she does all day for free. Just listen. The drop-off is at six o'clock in the morning, and the old guy leaves about six-thirty. Now, what do you think he'll do if he hears a noise outside his room, and

29

looks out to see Tina bent over the hood of a car, in a mini-skirt? If he doesn't have a heart attack, he'll for sure come out to see what her problem is. We'll be wearing masks. We grab him, hustle him back inside, tie him up, grab the money, and disappear. Brilliant, or what?"

"Is Tina going to be wearing a mask?" I ask. It seemed like the weak point in his plan.

"What, on her ass? She'll be bent over facing away from him. We'll have the old guy back in the room in seconds. I've got it all covered. All it takes is balls. You in, or what?"

When I don't answer right away, Jordan says, "Tell you what, let's take a walk, I'll show you the set-up. You'll feel better when you see what it looks like."

"Okay, I'm in," I decide, thinking about the steak I just had to steal.

Chapter 4

Jordan and I walk through town, headed toward the motel, when something else comes to mind.

"You say this guy's from Quebec, right?" I say.

"Must be. The car's from Quebec."

"That could mean bikers. They're big in Quebec. I read about them in the paper. They don't fool around. They kill people if they even suspect something's not right. Might not be the kind of guys we want to mess with, you think?"

"I don't plan on getting caught, and who's going to suspect *us* anyway?" he says.

"Still, it sounds dangerous and —"

Jordan suddenly grabs my arm and yanks me into an alley. He sticks his head out and looks in the direction of the Helmsdale police station.

"Check that out," he says. "Don't let him see you."

I ease my head out far enough to see Mr. Tarver

coming down the station steps and heading toward his car. He has a smug look on his face, and I assume that he's there to help the cops take us down. I feel like walking over to him and slamming him in the teeth.

"What do you figure?" Jordan asks.

"What do you think I figure?" I say. "Do you see that look on his face? I bet he's helping them nail us for what happened at school yesterday. His classroom faces the school parking lot. Now we've got him, the school's hockey heroes, and their rich prick parents lined up against us. There's a guy who'll wake up tomorrow morning with four flat tires on his car, that's what I figure."

"That's the spirit. We'll teach him not to stick his nose where it doesn't belong. Come on, I'll show you the set-up, then I got to go to Tanya's place for a while. Her folks are away until seven, you know what I'm saying?"

"Yeah, I hear you. You're playing it safe, right?" I ask, which makes him laugh.

"Oh yeah, I'll be gone by six, I figure that's pretty safe, right? Can't catch a guy who's got an hour head start on you."

We walk through town, skirting the parking lot of Bateman's Motel, past room number six, which is right around the corner from an alley. Jordan points out a short privacy wall that sticks out to the right of each room's door, but since room number six is the last one in line, it doesn't have one.

"See, number six is the last room, so when one

32

of us slips around the corner and grabs the old boy, the other can rush out from behind that little wall from room five for backup. Tina can take off, and we'll be gone in no time. Right down that alley, over the fence, and down to the brook through the woods. Just like we were never there."

"What about a licence plate?" I ask. "We going to steal one?"

"For Tina? We don't have to," he replies. "Her car will be parked in front of the door. When he opens it, he'll be looking at the side of her car, and her ass, so he'll never see the plate. I've got it covered, Eli. Let's just do it. We'll be set."

"Okay. When?" I ask. I'm starting to get jacked for the plan now, thinking about all that money.

"Last Sunday of this month," he says. "Welfare will be out on a Friday, so besides the regular suckers who dump their cash into the gambling machines, the welfare cases will be blowing their money too. Okay, so that's it. Let's get out of here, no need to hang out and get recognized. Shit, I forgot my weed at home."

∗∗∗

We've just walked through the door at Jordan's when the phone rings.

"Hello?" Jordan says. "No, she's at work right now . . . Yes, it is . . ." There's a long pause before he speaks again, "Yeah, I got it." He hangs up without saying goodbye.

He turns to me, smiling, and says, "Well, it looks like we're working men now. That was the school. We've been suspended indefinitely. 'Zero tolerance for violence policy' and all that crap. I guess I'll call Hank, see if he can use us."

Hank owns a construction company, and is Jordan's uncle. He hires us for weekend work sometimes — mostly demolition and lugging stuff around. The pay is good, and it keeps us in weed and cigarettes.

"Okay, he'll pick us up at seven tomorrow morning," Jordan says after hanging up. "Now I've got to get going. I'm late for Tanya's."

Jordan's mom will be home before he gets back tonight, so I decide to head over to the pool hall. Mrs. Black is nice enough to let me stay over when I need to, but I try to stay out of her way as much as I can. But before I go, I visit Jordan's room to get what I need to take care of that rat Tarver. I stumble over piles of dirty clothes to Jordan's bed and lift up a corner of the mattress. Lying there is Jordan's knife. It's short-bladed and sharp, perfect for what I need. I catch a glimpse of something else, and when I lift the mattress higher to check it out, I discover a small chrome handgun. I quickly drop the mattress, wondering where in hell he got it from, and why he hasn't told me about it.

***

I get a hero's welcome when I walk into Sniper Sam's pool hall. Most of the guys who hang out there don't like well-off jocks any more than Jordan or I do. Eric Mercer, who got slapped around by Tommy at a school dance one time, gives me a gram of hash as a reward.

"You better hope you don't get Judge Cameron," Winky Lawson tells me as I chalk up a cue-stick.

"Oh yeah? Why's that?" I ask.

"Because he and Cody's old man are buddies," he says. "They just bought the Barrington Arms Hotel. They're going to turn it into apartments. He'll bury your asses for sure."

"Whatever," I say, hiding the sick feeling that his news gives me. In a small town, things can really get bad if you mess with the wrong people, especially when you're a nobody. Maybe Jordan and I should think about skipping town with the money from the takedown before our court date.

I win two games, drop the third, then hang around until it's dark enough to head for Mr. Tarver's place. I stroll down his street, glad to see he doesn't have his outdoor light on. After circling the block, I cut through a backyard, and sneak up on his car, using his neighbour's hedge as cover. I'm trembling with excitement as I pull the knife out of my pocket.

A simple twist and push penetrates the wall of the first tire. I crawl around the car and do the other three. By the time I'm finished, the combined hissing noise from four punctured tires sounds like it could be heard all over town. I picture the cops sitting at Tim Horton's saying, "You hear that? Sounds like Mr. Tarver's tires being punctured. Oh well, I think I'll have another Boston Cream."

When I get back to Jordan's that night, his mother tells me he's already gone to bed. She says he seemed upset. I wonder if Tanya's parents came home early and caught him at their house. They're not exactly impressed with her choice of a boy-friend, and they go out of their way to make sure he knows he isn't welcome.

I'm hanging up my jacket when Jordan's little sister Kayla appears. She's thirteen, but thinks she's twenty. The kid dresses like a prostitute, and is always acting all flirty with me.

"Hey there," she says, striking a pose that makes my skin crawl. I wonder why her mother isn't straightening her out, but figure she's prob-ably too worried about Jordan's shit to notice what Kayla's up to.

"I'm going to hit the couch. Hank's picking us up at seven for work," I say.

"Yes, Jordan told me. That's just great," Mrs. Black says. I know sarcasm when I hear it.

I grab a blanket and pillow from the hall clos-et, and have just gotten comfortable when Kayla reappears, announcing that she's going to watch some videos.

It's her house, so I can't say much. She starts singing along to some song about girls being free to be who they wanted to be. I pop an eye open to find her mimicking the dance moves of the video

36

sluts, who are barely dressed and making no pretence about what they're trying to say with their
bodies. It's not that I don't normally like this stuff
— I do. Just not when it involves a thirteen-year-
old who's got the hots for me.

"I'm trying to sleep," I grunt.

"I'm trying to dance," she says.

I turn to face the back of the couch. Since I can't
sleep, I get to thinking. I'm seventeen years old,
and probably going to some kind of juvenile jail in
a few weeks. I smoke weed pretty well full time,
and am barely sliding by in school. My mom is
home drunk, and I'm sleeping on my best friend's
couch. My father is out there somewhere, maybe in
prison for all I know, and hasn't contacted me once
since he abandoned us. I'd just slashed the tires on
my teacher's car because I *guessed* he might be doing me a wrong turn, and soon I was going to rip
off what might be a biker organization.

I fall asleep wondering if maybe it's time to
change a few things in my life.

Chapter 5

"Six-thirty," Jordan says, kicking the couch to wake me up. "Coffee's on. I'll be outside. Hurry up."

Five minutes later I'm standing outside with a coffee in one hand and a hash joint in the other. Jordan is really quiet. Something is still bothering him. Maybe Tanya's parents finally got through to her and she dumped him. I don't ask.

Hank rolls up right on time and we drive to the area known as The Heights. It's a hill overlooking the river on the outskirts of town where all the big-shots have their mansions. Tennis courts, swimming pools, three-car garages. We pull into a yard paved with interlocking stone, and there's a Mercedes-Benz idling in an open door of the garage.

"This driveway, those walkways, everything you see that's stone, it's all got to go," Hank says as we get out. "We're redoing the roof, and the stone won't match the new colour, so they're replacing it.

Thank God for people with too much money, eh?"

"They couldn't find a shingle colour to match the stone? Or they couldn't replace the roof with the same-coloured shingles as before?" I ask.

"There's nothing wrong with the roof. It's only four years old," he explains. "Like I said, too much money. Figure they got to spend it somehow. All the better for us."

I can't imagine having so much money that I'd spend a fortune on *anything* just because I can. Maybe they can't sleep at night if the roof doesn't match the Benz.

The guy who owns the house comes out dressed in a slick three-piece suit, his snow-white hair and moustache perfectly groomed. He has a briefcase in one hand, and shoots the cuff on the other to check his dazzling gold watch as he approaches us.

"Hank, how are you?" he asks in one of those voices designed to sound impressive. He looks Jordan and me up and down like he already suspects us of something. And, like most people when they first meet me, his eyes linger a little too long as he tries to figure out what I am.

"Chindian," Jordan says.

"I'm Elias. This is Jordan," I say, offering my hand. The guy shakes it limply, then Jordan's, before casually wiping his palm on the leg of his pants. I picture myself carving something interesting on the side of his car with a screwdriver.

"Well, gentlemen, have a good day," he says,

quickly looking away. "As I was saying, Hank, if you can make use of that stone, feel free. I'll see you this evening."

"What does he do?" I ask Hank, as the Mercedes purrs out the driveway.

"Bank executive," he answers. "Nice guy, actually."

"Probably never did a day's work in his life," Jordan sneers.

"Speaking of a day's work, grab a ladder and a couple of roof rakes. We'll get started on stripping that baby. There's a whole day's work for two men right there."

There are about a dozen sections to the roof, so Jordan and Hank start at the top, stripping the shingles and throwing them down to the next level, where I toss them onto the ground. Within an hour, the rest of the crew lands, and with six of us working, we have a third of the roof stripped by coffee break.

Hank has made a run to Tim Horton's, so we all sit around eating donuts and drinking coffee. Except for Jordan, who goes off and sits by himself out behind the house.

"See the daughter?" Rob Calloway, an older guy with a huge belly, asks me with a leer.

"No," I say, thinking what a creep he is. Older guys talking about young girls grosses me out.

"Wouldn't mind nailin' that, what?" he goes on.

"Rob," Hank warns, shaking his head.

"Just jokin'," he claims.

"My daughter's the same age," Hank says, putting an end to it.

"What's wrong with Jordan?" Hank asks, turning to me. "He not feeling good?"

"I think him and Tanya had a fight or something," I tell him.

Just then the sanitation truck arrives with a dumpster for the discarded roofing. It's followed soon after by the delivery guys dropping off the new shingles.

"Okay, let's get at it," Hank says, and everyone swings into action. Two guys start reshingling the sections of roof we've already stripped, while Rob and I continue stripping. Jordan gets busy throwing shingles into the dumpster. As I watch him work, I can't help wondering what's bugging him.

Maybe his dad called. It seems like every time he does, Jordan is pissed off for days. Jordan's dad remarried and bought a place over in Grantsville, where he lives with his new wife and two daughters. They live much better than Jordan and Kayla do.

By lunchtime it's warm enough that everyone is stripped down to T-shirts, and the early summer sun feels good on my back. Jordan takes off by himself again, and I decide to check on him. I take a seat beside him on the stone wall overlooking a massive in-ground swimming pool.

"Must be nice," I say.

"Yeah."

"He's a banker," I add.

"I know. I'm not deaf," he says.

I can tell that Jordan isn't going to open up any-time soon, so I decide to amble back to sit with the rest of the crew instead of wasting my whole lunch break. Just as I'm crossing to the path that leads back to the trucks, I see the daughter Rob was talking about. I instantly recognize her from school. She graduated last year, a cheerleader and an honour student. She's beautiful and, for some reason, she seems excited to see me.

"Hi! You're Elias, right?" she says, flashing me a perfect smile. "I remember you from school."

"Uh, you too," I say, surprised.

"Hey, do you think you could give me a hand with something?" she asks, lifting the plastic shop-ping bag she's carrying. "My dad got me these new wipers for my car, but he didn't have time to put them on before he left this morning. I'm heading back to university for a few days, in Myerton, and I'm afraid it will rain before I get there."

"I . . . yeah, I'll try," I say.

The walkway is only wide enough for one per-son, so she's in front leading the way to the garage. Her figure, in tight stretchy pants and a crop-top, and the delicate scent that trails off her as she walks, makes me weak in the knees. Halfway there she turns her head and smiles at me. I hope she didn't notice where I'd been staring.

I follow her into the garage, and then the fun begins. She has her own car, a bright blue Cobalt with her name on the front licence plate: Amber.

First I try to pull the old wipers off by hand. Nothing doing. Then I find a screwdriver and try to twist what I think is a retainer clip loose from the wiper arm. Again, no luck. I'm starting to get embarrassed.

I'm getting frustrated because I figure I look like a fool. Then I realize that I've probably been going about it backwards. If the wiper blades pull *off*, they might come off when they're in use. But if they pull *on*, they'll stay put under pressure.

"Can you hold this?" I ask, holding the wiper arm up from the windshield.

"Sure," she says.

To do that, she has to stand facing me. She's almost right up against me as I push down on the blade. It still doesn't move. I push harder.

"Maybe you're not holding your face right," she says with a giggle. "My dad always says that. Try doing this."

She wrinkles her nose, puckers her lips, and crosses her eyes. We both burst out laughing, and suddenly the blade snaps free.

"Apparently *you* weren't holding *your* face right," I say.

We move to the other side, and the second one comes off easy. What *isn't* easy is standing that close to Amber without letting my mind wander into dangerous territory.

***

When I rejoin the rest of the crew, I'm smiling — until Lee Thompson asks why me and Jordan aren't in school.

"Got in a bit of a racket. Now we're kicked out for a while," I admit.

"Oh yeah? You the guys who jumped the Morgan kid?" he asks. "My young lad was telling me about it."

"We didn't jump anyone. It was a fair fight. Five of them and two of us."

"No kidding?" he says. "You must take after your old man. Now there was a guy you didn't want to get on the wrong side of. I seen him beat three guys at the old Legion one night. Took a beer bottle in the head and just kept on swinging. What's he doing now?"

"I wouldn't know. Haven't seen him since he took off when I was four," I tell him. My good mood from being close to Amber in the garage is evaporating.

"Oh, sorry," he says, looking away.

"Don't be."

"Okay boys, maybe we'd better concentrate on finishing what we've got stripped. The weather report says it might rain overnight," Hank tells us when break is over. "Elias, you and Jordan can start removing that stone, beginning down by the pool. We'll work our way back."

We take turns lifting the stones and piling them into a wheelbarrow, then stacking them up neatly beside the garage. I enjoy the work, and the way it

44

pumps my muscles up. I'm thinking I don't care if I ever go back to school. Then I remember *why* I'm not in school, and what's probably ahead for me, and then the fun goes out of it.

Chapter 6

"A good day, boys," Hank says, signalling the end of another work day. "If the weather cooperates, we should have that roof finished in another two days."

I'm impressed, as always, by the fact that Hank has worked just as hard as anyone else. He'd even lugged bundles of shingles up the ladder to the roof, which had left my legs trembling from the effort. And he's twenty-five years older than me.

On the way home Hank pays us for some work we did last weekend, when we shovelled two truckloads of crushed stone into a basement. It took us over ten hours of non-stop labour, but it was a good workout, and well worth the hundred bucks he paid each of us.

There's no one home at Jordan's place, so we smoke a joint and kick back in the living room. Jordan is still not saying much. I can't think of anything to say either. So I just sit there figuring out what I'm going to do with all the money I'll be making.

It doesn't take long. We always have more bills coming in than we can pay, and I'm thinking it might be a good idea to just forget about school. I'll probably never go to trade school anyway, and I can learn everything I need to know about construction from Hank and his guys. Hank never finished high-school, and he does all right.

"Maybe you should go home," Jordan says, breaking into my thoughts.

"Yeah, I need to grab some clean clothes anyway. You want to go shoot some pool later?"

"No, I mean maybe you should go home, you know, and stay there. Enough's enough. We can't help it if your mom's a lush. It's crowded enough here as it is."

My temper flares, but I force it down. Jordan and me have always gotten along, and I know something's been eating at him. He's about the last person I ever want to mess with, so I do the smart thing. I swallow my pride and agree with him.

"Yeah, you're right. This has been going on too long. I'll see you in the morning," I say, getting up to leave.

"So you don't want to shoot pool now? You all upset because I asked you to live at your own house?" he asks, tipping his chin up in the air the way he does when he's ready to fight.

"Jordan, if you want, I'll go shoot some pool.

You just said no. Look, I can see you're upset about something, but unless your problem is with me, I got nothing to say, okay? I'll just go home. It's not that big a deal."

"Sorry, man," he says, finally. "I'll meet you at Sam's later, I got a stop to make first."

***

Mom is sitting at the table with a cup of coffee in front of her when I get home. It can't have been too long since she had a drink though, because she's slurring her words when she speaks.

"How was school?" she asks.

"Good," I lie.

"I forgot about supper. I was busy," she tells me. One look at the place and I can see that she wasn't busy cleaning.

"I already ate," I lie again. I shower, then walk down to the drugstore and put eighty bucks on our power bill. The girl behind the counter raises an eyebrow at the total on the bill. Then she looks at me like I owe *her* the money.

"You got a problem?" I ask.

"I got no problem," she says, snapping her gum in dismissal.

"Let me speak to whoever's in charge here," I demand.

"What?" she asks.

"You deaf, or just stupid?" I ask her. "Let me speak to the manager. Now."

"Uh, he's not around," she says.

"Who's in charge here?" I ask, maybe a bit too loud.

"Excuse me, what's the problem?" I hear a woman's voice say. I turn to see a middle-aged woman in a white smock walking toward me.

"Are you in charge?" I ask.

"Well, I'm the pharmacist. So yes, I guess I am right now. Is there something I can help you with?"

"This stupid bitch . . . with her gum . . ." I say, but then the woman cuts me off.

"Just calm down. What seems to be the problem?" she says.

"I just want to pay this god-damned bill! I don't need people looking at me as if I'm trash, okay?!" I suddenly realize that everyone in the store is staring at me. One of them is Jordan. I slam the money down on the counter and wait for my receipt, breathing slowly and deeply. Seeing Jordan makes me realize that I'm acting just like he would, and I've never understood that behaviour before. I thank the girl, who ignores me, and leave.

I cross the street to the sub shop and get myself a meatball sandwich, then plunk down on the retaining wall outside and eat it. I'm thinking that maybe I should go home and pile some firewood instead of shooting pool. Maybe it'll help me calm down. I look up and see Jordan leaving the drug store.

"Hey," he says, slipping something into his pocket as he crosses the street.

"What's up?" I ask.

"Just heading to Tanya's for a minute, then over to Sam's to shoot pool. See you there?" he says.

"Actually, I think I'd better get some firewood in. It's good and dry now, and it'll be full of snakes and mice if I leave it out much longer. I'll catch you in the morning," I say, standing to leave.

"I'll come over in a while and give you a hand," he tells me. There's an awkward silence before Jordan continues. "Look, about before . . . It's just that Tanya's driving me nuts. You know you can stay at our place as long as you want, all right?"

"I don't know. Thanks, but I think it's about time I took care of some things."

The scene in the drugstore is still fresh in my mind, and I think that maybe I've let Jordan be too much of an influence on me. Maybe it's time to start being my own man.

"Your call. Anyway, I'll stop at Matthew's place. I hear he got a new delivery. We'll get ourselves above it all," he says. "Way above."

I go back home and start pitching wood in through the basement window. I hope Mom is passed out again. Not because I like to see her smashed. I'm just not in the mood to listen to her right now.

I throw wood until it's piled right up to the level of the window. As I do, I think that maybe I should do more to help Mom out, instead of just running away from her every month.

I go in to stack. Passing through the kitchen,

I hear Mom's voice from the living room, and I wonder who she's talking to. I slip quietly over to the archway that separates the rooms, and peek around the corner. She's on the phone.

"I worry about him," she's saying. "And that Jordan, he's no help, that's for sure. It's a hard world, Rose. I'm afraid he's headed down the same path as his father."

There's a pause and I turn to walk away, but not in time.

"No, I never did," Mom says. "I always meant to, but I'm afraid of how he'll react. I mean, isn't it better for him to think that his father just disappeared? That maybe he'll come back, or even call some day? I don't know, Rose. I just don't want to think about it. Anyway, I've got to go."

I step around the corner just as she's hanging up the phone. She takes one look at me, and it must have been written all over my face that I heard, because she bursts into tears and covers her face with her hands.

"What happened to him?" I demand.

The question just makes her cry even harder. I stand there watching, waiting for an answer. I've spent my whole life thinking my father walked out on us and never looked back. Now I want the truth.

"Well?" I repeat as she starts to get control of herself. She reaches for the half-full vodka bottle on the coffee table. I rush over to take it from her. She grabs it and tucks it under her arm like a little kid.

"Give it to me," I say through clenched teeth.

"No. Please?" she begs.

"Give me that fucking bottle," I seethe. She's shocked to hear me speak to her like that, but I'm not about to apologize.

When she refuses to pass it over, I lean forward and yank it away from her. In one move she's on her feet and swinging her hand at my head. I close my eyes as she lands a stinging slap flush on my cheek. In my world you hit back, and my fist is nearly to her face when I somehow stop it, causing me to lose my balance and crash into her. She falls back onto the couch, cowering, both arms wrapped around her head.

"Please, no, Heath," she whines. My stomach lurches as I connect the frightened woman and my father together.

Suddenly I'm exhausted. It's the same feeling as when I've had a short but brutal street brawl. I want to say I'm sorry, but I want away from her more. Walking to the kitchen, I intend to pour the booze down the sink. Instead, I set it on the counter. Returning to the living room, I find her sitting with her arms wrapped tightly around herself, rocking back and forth, staring straight ahead.

"The truth." I choke out the words. "You can drink yourself to death if you want. But first you'll tell me what really happened to my dad."

"He's gone," she says. "When he left, he was supposed to go to work in the mines, in Ontario. He was going to send us money, make sure we were provided for. Somehow he ended up in Manitoba. Him and some other guys robbed a liquor store, but they didn't get far. He got four years in the penitentiary. Three weeks after he went in he was stabbed to death."

My father is dead.

After all the years of silently waiting for a call, a letter, or a visit, there it is.

There's only one question left to ask. "*Why?* Why did you lie to me all those years?"

She starts bawling again. I fight the urge to walk away, and at last she pulls herself together enough to answer.

"I was nine when my own father died," she says. Her head is down and tears are still falling, but her voice is steady. "I knew I had to tell you the truth someday, but every time I thought about losing my own dad, I couldn't bring myself to do it. It was the worst thing that ever happened to me, losing him. It left me lost and empty."

I stay silent, letting her hurt.

"The hardest thing about death is that it doesn't leave a shred of hope. It's so final. And when I got the news that Heath was gone, I couldn't tell you, because I couldn't bear to do that to you. You were only four years old, Elias. Please understand."

"So instead you let me think he took off and never looked back?"

Mom shakes her head back and forth, like she's trying to puzzle it out. "Every time I thought I had found the courage to tell you, I pictured how devastated you would be. The years just slipped by. You quit asking, and it became easier to just say nothing."

"I quit asking, but I never quit wondering," I say, turning away. "Your booze is on the counter."

"I'm so sorry, Eli," she cries after me. "Can you ever forgive me?"

I ignore her question.

"I have wood to pile," I say as I head for the door. I try not to think about my father lying on a cold cement floor as his life leaked away from him, but the image won't leave my brain. I wonder if he thought about me as he died.

I'm sitting on the woodpile, still fighting back tears, when Jordan shows up. He doesn't say a word, but lights a joint and hands it to me.

For a while we sit in silence, my mind so full of thoughts I can't focus on any one of them. Every time I try, another one comes rushing at me, until I feel like my brain is going to unravel. I need to be alone. I tell Jordan I'm done for the night.

"I'll see you in the morning then," he says. "You want to call Hank, get him to pick you up here?" He's looking at the ground as he says it, and I know he's feeling bad about kicking me out earlier.

"Yeah, I'll do that," I say, not willing to let him off the hook just yet.

I watch him walk away with his head down and his shoulders slumped. Part of me still wishes that I could ask him what it is that's bothering him, but I know there's no point.

Chapter 7

Mom is still sleeping when I get up for work early the next morning. I had lain awake for hours the night before, wondering what life would've been like if Dad had lived. Maybe his time in prison would've made him realize what was important, like being around to raise his son. I finally came to the conclusion that none of it really matters. It's over and done with, and has been for a long time.

When I walk into the kitchen, I'm surprised to find it sparkling clean. Mom must have been up half the night scrubbing and scouring.

I forgot to call Hank last night. I don't want to take a chance on waking anyone up by phoning, so I walk over to Jordan's place.

I get there early. When Jordan comes out he asks me why I didn't come inside and wait. He sparks up a joint, but I refuse it.

"Whoa, going straight, or what?" Jordan asks,

holding the joint out again.

It's not just that I'm in a bad mood about last night, but I don't like being all jammed up around other people. It's the opposite effect than what I'm looking for.

"Maybe later," I tell him.

"Your choice," he says.

Hank pulls up, and we pile into the truck with him. He has coffee for us, and I start to feel a little better. Like a man, heading out to do a man's work.

"Crack your window, Eli," Hank says as we drive away. "You guys smell like a skunk took a leak on you."

Jordan snickers. I wish I could tell Hank it wasn't me.

"Try to stay away from Layton. He smells that crap on you guys, he's not going to like it," Hank says as we pull up to the job site.

"What's his problem?" Jordan asks.

"Listen, don't assume he has a problem, okay?" Hank says. "It's just not exactly good for business to show up at a man's house smelling like weed, you understand? Pretend you have a little respect, okay?"

Jordan doesn't answer right away, but Hank isn't letting it go. "I asked you a question," he says.

"Yeah, I got it," Jordan mumbles.

The day goes by quickly, because we're busy. Just before we quit, I ask Hank if I can take some undamaged shingles out of the dumpster to fix my roof at home.

"Never mind that," he says. "I'll have the boys drop by and fix it for you. We always have extra shingles, and it'll only take them a few minutes."

He slaps me on the shoulder, like I'm one of the guys. I like the feeling it gives me.

***

When I get home I open the door to the smell of something that makes my mouth water. Mom is standing by the stove, looking proud.

"Lasagne. Your favourite," she says with a nervous smile. "You're late. How was school? And why are you so dirty?"

I consider putting off telling the truth until later, but we've had enough of that in our lives. I need something to change, and this seems like a good place to start.

"We need to talk," I tell her, taking a seat at the table.

"Oh, Eli. I know I should have told you about your father sooner, but it was just so easy to keep putting it off," she says, pulling out a chair.

"No. Not that," I say, knowing that it will be a while before I'm ready to talk to her about it again. I realize that, although my father has been dead for a long time, the loss is brand-new to me. At the moment, all I really feel is numb.

"Jordan and I got into some trouble at school," I continue. "A fight — with some guys from the hockey team. They started it . . ."

I stop myself. Actually, they hadn't started anything. Jordan had started the whole thing, because he thought someone had looked at him the wrong way. He started it because he couldn't back off and walk away. Of course, I'd been just as bad, getting all worked up when I realized what was about to go down.

"And . . . ?" Mom looks like she knows it isn't something that will be easy to deal with. She reaches up to brush a stray strand of hair from her face, and I can see that her hand is trembling. Alcohol withdrawal.

"Jordan broke a guy's jaw. I cut a guy real bad. With my fist, I mean. His eyebrow. We're being charged with aggravated assault. We're also kicked out of school, probably for the rest of the term. I think we might get time, like reform school, or a group home, or juvie, or something. The other guys say we jumped them for no reason. Their friends back them up, of course, and we've got no witnesses on our side. So, there it is. I'm sorry."

Mom's eyes are wet, but she keeps from crying. I'm glad. I don't think I can handle that right now.

"Maybe they'll change their minds," she says. "Maybe they'll tell the truth once they get to court?"

"I don't think so. It's the same old story. They're rich, we're poor, no one cares about the truth." Once the words are out, I realize just how true they are.

The oven buzzer goes and she gets up and gets us both a plate full of lasagne. I don't feel much like eating. It looks like she doesn't either. We push the food around our plates, nibble a bit, and comment on how good it is. But not much gets eaten.

"I'm working with Hank. That will be a help," I say.

Mom nods but says nothing.

Finally I can't take not talking about what we both must be thinking. "Where's Dad buried, Mom?"

"Dauphin, Manitoba." She drops the fork into her half-finished supper. "His mother moved out there before you were born. She claimed the . . . his body. Maybe you and I could go out there too, someday."

"Yeah," I say. "Maybe."

She leaves the table then, and I hear her bed-room door close. I scrape my supper into the gar-bage and go outside for a smoke. Now that the firewood is in, my next task will be to rake up the leaves from last fall. I feel the need to keep myself busy, so I walk down to the grocery store to buy bags for the leaves.

I'll pack the leaves in garbage bags and stack them in the backyard until fall. Then I'll stack them tightly against the foundation walls, for in-sulation. If I don't, the old stone walls let out so much heat that the snow against them melts. Then cold air pours in, and the floors feel like ice, even if you're wearing slippers.

Jordan is waiting for me when I get back. He's standing in my yard with his hands shoved deep into his jacket pockets. With a cigarette dangling from the corner of his mouth, he reminds me of those old posters of James Dean, from back when smoking was cool. He's staring straight ahead, like he's lost in thought. Maybe it's the thought of going to jail that's freaking him out, too.

"Hey, what's happening?" I ask, snapping him out of it.

"Tanya," he says. He shakes his head and sighs deeply. "Tanya's pregnant."

Chapter 8

It takes a minute before the reality of what he says sinks in. I'm glad it's not me in that position. Neither of us is exactly Daddy material.

"Are you sure?" I finally ask.

"Yeah, *really* sure. She took two pregnancy tests," he says.

"So, what are you going to do?" I ask.

"I'm going to be a father, that's what I'm going to do," he says.

"Really?" I say. It's hard to picture Jordan as a father.

"You think I'd make this up? She took two pregnancy tests, passed them both. Or failed them both . . . I guess it's all how you look at it. So we're going to have a baby."

"Her folks know?" I ask.

"This weekend. We'll tell them this weekend. That should go over big. I'm ready, Eli. I've thought it over. Tanya wants to keep it, so that's it. We'll be having a kid. That takedown I got planned is going to come in really handy now."

"I've been thinking about that," I say. "Maybe we should try to straighten out this mess we're in first. It'll still be there, right? That's not going to change."

"No, it goes down as planned. I need that money," he says, shifting his weight back and forth from one foot to the other. He's rolling his head around like he's got a kink in his neck, and he spits every few seconds. "I'm thinking maybe I'll skip. Take Tanya and head out West. I'll do the takedown myself, if I can't count on you."

"Okay, I'll do it," I say. Suddenly it's pissing me off that all he has to do is make me feel like I'm letting him down for me to cave. I feel trapped. Jordan's confident he's got it nailed, but if anything goes wrong, it won't be like the other chances we've taken.

"What are you doing now?" I ask him.

"Just trying to keep it together," he replies. "You?"

"I was going to rake up the leaves, or get a start at least. You want to hold the bags for me? Then we can go shoot a few games, okay?"

"Sure," he says. "I need a break from Tanya anyway. She can't stop crying, and it's getting a little old. Women, eh?"

Pregnant women, I think. Or more like pregnant girls. Tanya's only sixteen, and I can't imagine how scared she must be.

"Yeah, well, you're not the one who's pregnant," I tell him.

"I know," he says. "And she was on the Pill, too. Or so she said."

"Don't be a jerk, Jordan," I say. "You think she'd be crying full time if she did it on purpose? Birth-control pills are only ninety-some-percent reliable. You knew that, right?"

"Yeah, I guess. But watch who you're calling a jerk, jerk," he replies.

We eyeball each other for a second but, as usual, I back down. I go to the shed for a rake, and he follows me inside. When I turn around he's lighting another joint.

"No thanks," I say when he offers me a hit.

"Suit yourself," he says, sucking on the joint so hard I can see it collapsing in on itself.

***

It's only Thursday night, and there aren't many people around the pool hall, just the usual guys who hang out there all the time. We shoot a game of doubles with the Darwin brothers, then Jordan goes outside with them to get high. I've just racked up the balls, and I'm practising bank shots with the cue ball, when I happen to look out the window.

I see Jordan talking to this guy with long hair and a goatee. There's trouble brewing. I can see it in their body language. I ease over to the door to check things out, still holding the pool cue.

There are actually three guys, and they have Jordan sort of surrounded. The Darwin boys, who are basically simple-minded and harmless, are standing back a way. They're waiting for the show.

I recognize the guys who are squaring off with Jordan. They're just some morons who live out in the sticks and like to pick fights when they've had a few drinks. They drive an old Ford LTD, with dice hanging from the rear-view mirror and little purple lights mounted around the windshield. I still haven't figured out what decade they're lost in. What I do know is that they think nothing of putting the boots to someone.

Sam, who runs the pool hall, is dozing behind his desk, way back in the corner, out of view of the sidewalk. I open the door and step outside.

"Here's another faggot," goatee guy says. I can smell booze in the air. Then I see the knife in his hand.

"Just in time to see your girlfriend go down," he says as he moves toward Jordan.

His buddies think this is pretty clever, and are still laughing when I step forward and swing the cue at his head. He ducks, but I reverse my swing as he straightens up. The cue catches him on the bridge of the nose, sending a spray of blood flying. His knife falls to the sidewalk as he staggers backwards, holding his face with both hands.

One of his buddies makes a grab for the knife and, just as he gets his hand on it, Jordan stomps down on it with his heel. There's a wet crunching noise, and the guy screams in pain as he jumps back, holding his hand up in front of him. I'd say there are at least two broken fingers.

I pick up the knife and whip it across the street into a vacant lot. They all bail into the car and the only one who isn't injured takes the wheel. As they pull away in a cloud of tire smoke, he holds his hand up like he's aiming a gun at me. I spit in his general direction.

"Cool," Harvey, the least simple of the Darwin brothers says.

"Come on, let's get out of here," I say to Jordan. "We don't need any more trouble."

We cut through the back streets behind the pool hall, and stop a few blocks away, in the loading dock of an abandoned warehouse. I pull out a cigarette and lean against the wall, trembling so hard that I have a hard time getting my lighter to work.

"What a rush, eh?" Jordan says.

"A rush? You could've been killed. That guy was moving on you with a knife. What happened back there?" I ask, although I already know the answer.

"Those guys are assholes. They think they're tough, with their stupid long hair and leather jackets. I just mentioned it to them, that's all."

"That's all? You thought you'd start something with three guys, that's all? What if I hadn't looked out the window? What if I'd gone to the bathroom? You could be lying on the pavement, dead. *That's all.*"

"I had it under control," he replies. "I didn't need your help. Next time, just stand back and enjoy the action."

"You're over the edge, Jordan," I say. "You've got a kid coming, and we've got court coming, and maybe, *probably,* jail coming. You're going to end up like my old man."

"Like your old man?" he asks.

"Dead," I tell him.

"Your father's dead? Seriously? When did you find that out?"

"The other day," I say. "He was stabbed to death in prison when I was just a little kid. This shit is getting old, and I don't want to end up like that. You hear what I'm saying? This stopped being fun when we got arrested."

"I'm sorry, man," he says.

"Don't be," I tell him. I don't need anyone's pity. I turn around and walk away.

Chapter 9

I hardly get any sleep that night. I keep having dreams that jolt me awake, my adrenaline pumping like crazy. There are knives and cops, and cops with knives, and always someone waiting in the shadows for me. I think that maybe it's my father, that maybe he isn't really dead, that he just wanted people to think he was. Then I realize, too late, that it's actually someone waiting to take me down. I give up trying to sleep, finally, and get out of bed.

By the time Hank arrives, I've been up for three hours. I'm vibrating from four cups of coffee and half a dozen cigarettes. He takes one look at me and states the obvious: "Rough night?" He grins, and I know he's thinking I must have been partying.

"I guess," I reply.

"I remember those days, out most the night, living like a tomcat. Can't say I miss them, though. I never would have pictured myself being happy just staying home with a wife and kids, but I wouldn't trade it for the world. What's important to you changes — at least it does for some of us. But then again, some people never walk away. I worry about that nephew of mine and that attitude, you know?"

"I guess," I say. I know exactly what Hank means, but I'm not about to put down my best friend to him. Even though I'm still pissed off about the fix he got us into last night.

Hank has us all concentrating on finishing the roof, since he doesn't want to take any chances on leaving it open for the weekend. By three-thirty, the crew is nailing down the last of the ridge cap. Jordan and I start cleaning up the job site just as the homeowner pulls in.

"I'm going to fire up the barbecue," he says, coming out of the garage with his hands full of grocery bags. "Steaks will be ready in about half an hour."

"Sounds great," I say as he passes. I guess he's just trying to be one of the guys.

"Sounds great," Jordan mocks as the guy disappears into the house. "Why don't you just kiss his powdered ass?"

"What's wrong with you?" I ask him. "The guy's just being nice."

"He's just trying to show off. That's what he's doing. Thinks we never had steak in our lives. Well, he can shove it. I don't take charity. The guy's just another crook in an expensive suit."

I don't waste my time arguing, and Jordan borrows Hank's cellphone and calls a cab. When it arrives, he asks me if I'm coming.

"No," I say, noticing the blue Cobalt coming down the street.

We all have steaks and salad out on the back deck, and Mr. Layton, dressed in jeans and a sweatshirt now, seems like any other guy. His wife is really nice, too. And then Amber appears. She notices me sitting by the pool and makes her way over. She's in a short skirt and high heels. Just glancing at her legs gives me that weak feeling again, as if I'm suddenly not getting enough air into my lungs.

"Hey, Eli. How are you?" she asks. "Are you busy?"

I have no idea what she's up to, but it has to be something. Girls like Amber don't bother with guys like me unless they want something. I think back to helping her with her windshield wipers and can't help but wonder what she wants me to do now. Rotate her tires?

"Busy?" I say. "Not really. What do you need done?"

"Oh, no. Nothing else," she laughs. "But thanks for your help last week. I was just wondering if you wanted to go for a drive to the mall," she says, dazzling me with a smile. "Mom's birthday is tomorrow, and I still haven't gotten her a gift."

"I . . . guess so. Yeah, sure," I mumble. So I

end up at the mall with a beautiful rich girl, wandering from store to store as she searches for a gift for her mom's birthday. She keeps walking and standing too close to me. At least too close to me — for me. She's got to know what kind of effect she has on guys.

She finally settles on a lamp and pays for it with a credit card. As we're walking back to her car, her cellphone rings.

"Hi," she says. "No, I changed my mind. I got Elias to come with me instead. He's working at our house. He's been a sweetie, put up with me for two hours now."

There's a short silence.

"Yeah, Elias Minto. How many guys named Elias do you know?"

She finishes the call as we get to her car. We climb in and drive out onto the street as she puts her hand on my arm.

"Thank you so much, Elias," she says. "I had fun."

"Sure, me too," I say.

"Are you doing anything tomorrow night?" she asks.

"I'm not sure yet," I say, trying to act cool. "Why?"

"I've got this thing to go to. It's no big deal, but it would be nice if you would come along. None of my friends are up for it, I mean, not that we aren't friends, you and me, that is. Well, we don't really hang out, but still . . . I'm rambling now, huh?"

"I think you could call that rambling," I say. "What kind of thing is it?"

"The surprise birthday party for my mom. It'll be all older people, but I have to be there. If you came, we could get away early, maybe check out a movie or something. Am I being too pushy?" she says. Girls like her can be as pushy as they want to be, I figure.

"Well, no, and it could be fun, I guess," I say.

"Perfect!" she says. "You want me to pick you up?"

We're getting close to my neighbourhood, and just then it hits me. She lives in a mansion in the rich part of town, drives a fancy car, and is in university, preparing for a successful life. Then there's me. Unless I make some major changes, I'll never be more than what I am right now: a labourer. If I'm headed anywhere else, it's probably to a jail cell. As she turns onto my street the thought of her seeing where I live makes the decision for me.

"Hold it. I didn't say I was going," I tell her. "Pull over here."

"What?" she asks.

"I'm not going. Just pull over and let me out," I say. I have to get out of there.

It's a narrow street, so she hauls into the parking lot of a convenience store. As soon as the car stops, I get out and start walking. She drives around the lot and cuts me off just before I hit the sidewalk. The car comes to a stop right in front of me and her window is down.

"I don't understand," she begins. "Why —"

"Look, I know you don't, Amber," I say. "You don't because you can't." I turn and walk away and don't look back.

When I get home, Mom hands me an envelope that Hank has dropped off. It's my pay, in cash. I pocket a hundred bucks and give the rest to her, although I know that's usually not such a good idea. I really don't care at this moment. I just feel like getting wasted, so I call Jordan.

"Hey," he says. "There's a party at Butch Davidson's place. His parents are away for the night. I have to stop by Tanya's place, but I should make it to the party by nine. You want to do the thing and get me six beers and a pint of rum?"

The "thing" he's talking about is the slickest way we've figured out to get booze without hanging outside the liquor store bribing people of age to buy it for us. I call the taxi company Mom always uses, and they deliver whatever I order to my house — just like it's for Mom. Not that they care who it's for anyway, as long as they get paid.

I order Jordan's booze, plus six beers and a pint of whisky for myself. I watch for the cab and meet the driver in the yard, tipping him five bucks. As I'm putting the bottles into grocery bags, Mom comes into the kitchen.

"What's this?" she asks.

"It's not for you, so don't worry about it," I say.

Chapter 10

When I wake up the next morning, I'm curled up on a chair in Butch's living room. I can't remember much from the night before. There are beer bottles everywhere, and someone has puked on the floor in front of the TV. For all I know, it could've been me. A couple of guys are passed out on the couch, and one more on the floor in front of it.

I go into the bathroom to rinse my mouth out and have to step over a girl who's curled up around the toilet like it's her favourite teddy bear. I wonder if Amber and her spoiled friends party this hard.

On my way back down the hall, I see Jordan through an open bedroom door. He's sound asleep. Snuggled up next to Tina Bradley. Their clothes are scattered all over the room, so there isn't much doubt as to what had gone down. I can't help but feel sorry for Tanya. Still, I take a second look, just in case any parts of Tina aren't covered.

It's after nine o'clock. As I make my way home, the sun is shining brightly through the brilliant green leaves of the trees. Even the air seems to be green. Flowers are bursting out in outrageous colours everywhere I look, and the air is scented with a hint of lilac. I feel like I might puke.

I'm approaching my house when I see a cop car coming toward me. I quickly search my mind for anything that I might've done the night before, but it's all a drunken blank. I can only hope that the cop behind the wheel is just cruising. No such luck.

The black and white pulls into my yard. I fight the urge to turn and run. But the cops don't even look my way as the car backs out onto the street and tears off in the direction it came from, siren blaring and lights flashing.

Why am I being so paranoid? Is this what its going to be like from now on? I used to just hate cops, but now I find myself scared of them. I think about some of the older guys I know — burnouts who live their lives in the dark, always ducking someone.

I look around at the picket fence that runs around our property. It's rotted and crumbling. The steps aren't much better. The house used to be blue, but now it's faded to a blurry light-purple colour. The place is definitely worth being embarrassed about. Maybe if the score from the takedown is big enough, I can put a down payment on the place, then start renovating it. The thought of the takedown while I'm subject to the court undertaking makes me shiver.

I go inside and say hello to Mom, who is sitting on the couch holding a picture in her hands. She holds it up, facing me, as I walk over to check it out. Her hands are trembling, and I assume it's from alcohol withdrawal. As I get closer in the dim light, my first thought is that it's a picture of me.

It isn't. It's my dad, smiling at the camera, his arm around a younger version of Mom. Without her in the shot, I could be looking in the mirror.

"You can have this," she says, standing up. I put my arms around her as she sobs into my shoulder. By the time she's done, my T-shirt is damp where her head laid. I let go of her and go to my room, setting the picture on my dresser and changing into work clothes. Later I'll get the picture blown up and framed for my wall — a reminder that, although I might look like him, I don't have to turn out like he did.

After a quick bite to eat, I walk down to the hardware store and buy two cans of white Fisherman's Paint, and one of brown stain. Tommy's father serves me. He has no idea I'm the one who scarred his son for life. Next stop is the Dollar Store, where I get rollers, trays, and brushes.

I take it all back to my place in a taxi and go to work. With a wide brush, I paint a strip around the windows and both doors, then another just under the eaves. The paint is made for use on old, weathered, even rotted, boards, and does a great job of covering the house's cedar shingles. By the time I'm ready to start rolling, my hangover catches up to me, and I lie down on the grass for a few minutes to recover.

I've just gotten started when Jordan lands. He's stoned and in a foul mood, but I put him to work anyway. He doesn't mention last night or the fact that he woke up with someone other than his pregnant girlfriend. That's fine with me. I have enough shit of my own to deal with. Besides, it's not really my business. He'll do what he wants anyway.

"You were in great shape last night," he states.

"Yeah," I reply.

"I talked to Tina, everything's a go," he says.

"Talked to her, did you?" I say. He keeps painting, but says nothing.

In two hours we have the whole front and one side of the house finished, including the brown stain on the window trim. It looks amazing.

I grab us each a can of pop from the fridge and we sit on the step to take a break. Jordan's been quiet the whole time we were working. After a few more minutes of uncomfortable silence, I decide to give him an opening if he wants it.

"So, you talk to Tanya's folks?" I ask.

"Yeah," he says.

"And . . . ?"

"They want her to have an abortion. Said we've got no future. That we can't drag another kid up in poverty. That it wouldn't be right."

"But it's okay to kill it?" I ask.

"I guess they think so. Anyway, I'm not going to let that happen. I can work for Hank, maybe get my carpentry licence later on. I think Welfare will pay for an apartment for Tanya and the kid. It'll all work out. Besides, I've got at least a few grand coming my way from the takedown. That could set us up out West, if Tanya would agree to move. There's big money out there. You just have to go for it. Take a risk, you know?"

"What about court?" I remind him. "What if we get nailed on the takedown? What if we end up in jail?"

"Not much I can do about that. I'll get the lawyer to explain my situation to the judge. He'll probably just give me probation. And they can't send you to jail if they don't send me, right?"

"I guess not," I reply. I hope he's right, but I have my doubts. When you're on the bottom of the social ladder, the climb up to justice can be a long one.

"What, you losing your balls again?" he says.

"No, maybe I'm using my head, asshole," I say. He grits his teeth and stares at me, but this time I stare back. It's not too long before he puts his roller in the tray and walks off. I let him.

Chapter 11

I'm high up on the ladder when I hear a car horn from the driveway. I look down to see Amber sitting in her car, looking at me like she's a little scared. I climb down and walk over.

"Hi," she says, making it sound like a question.

I nod but say nothing.

"I want to talk to you . . . if you don't mind," she says.

"How did you know where I lived?"

"The Internet. There's only one Minto in town, so I drove over. Is that okay?"

She had to see the anger on my face, so she knew perfectly well that it wasn't okay. Even so, I didn't want to hurt her feelings. I'm not that big of an idiot.

"Yeah, I guess."

"You kind of look mad," she says.

"I'm not, though," I say, completely caving and

letting a smile come to my face. She's gorgeous.

"Can I get out?" she asks.

"Oh, yeah, sorry." I open her door and she steps out onto the dirt driveway. She tugs her shorts into place. I try not to stare.

"So you're painting the place. Cool," she says. "My dad never does any of that stuff."

"Yeah, well, I guess he doesn't have to, right?"

"He couldn't anyway. He's a total klutz," she says. "You know, it's not my fault I live in a fancy house, Elias. I mean, if that's what's bothering you."

"I know," I tell her. I'm now embarrassed by the way I acted the day before. She's right. It isn't her fault, any more than it's my fault I live in a dump. Maybe her being interested in me isn't so far-fetched, since the only big difference between us is our parents' income.

"Can I help?" she asks, nodding toward the half-painted house.

"Okay," I say. I'm thinking, why not? There's nothing to hide now. She's seen the place, and I could use some help.

"Great!" she exclaims. "I never get to do things like this."

I set her up with a roller and tray, and we start on the end wall that I haven't gotten to yet. I roll the upper part, and she rolls the lower. I have a hard time keeping my eyes off her when she bends over to load the roller, then stretches to paint.

"You're not looking at my bum, are you?" she asks suddenly, without turning around.

I burst out laughing and admit it. She laughs too, and it feels normal, like two friends having fun.

"So, bum-looker," she says, "about that lame party tonight?"

I'm sick of smoking weed and shooting pool, sick of the sameness of everything. Jordan's pissed off, and I'm not about to track him down and make everything better. I'm more than up for something different.

"Sure, why not? We can suffer together," I say. "And I promise not to look at your bum anymore."

"Yeah, but I bet you won't look at it any *less,* either," she says, threatening me with the roller. Then she does a little wiggle dance before dipping her roller into the tray and getting back to the painting. I think I might fall off the ladder.

We finish the wall, then she has to leave. I hate to see her go. She was a much better painting partner than Jordan.

"I'll pick you up at seven-thirty, okay?" she says as I walk her to her car.

"That's fine," I tell her. At the car, she turns to face me suddenly, and I find myself too close to her. For a split second I have the urge to lean forward and kiss her, but I don't quite have the nerve. She does.

"See you then," she says with a smile. She's long gone before I can't feel her lips on mine anymore.

***

I clean up the brushes and rollers, wipe the trays clean, and put everything away. With sunshine forecast for the next day, I'll easily be able to finish the back wall. Standing on the sidewalk looking at the job so far, I have a real feeling of accomplishment. It feels good.

"Who was that?" Mom asks when I go inside.

"Oh, a friend. Amber," I tell her.

"She's pretty," she says.

"Yeah, she is," I agree.

"Whose car?" she asks.

"Hers. Her dad is high up at the Toronto Dominion Bank."

"Must be nice," Mom says.

"I imagine," I say. "What's for supper?"

"Chops. Are you hungry?"

"A bit, but no hurry, I'm going to my room for a while. Amber's picking me up at seven-thirty. We might go to a movie. Actually, first we're going to her place. There's a birthday party for her mom. Are my good jeans clean?" I ask.

"They will be," she says with a smile. "I'll iron that nice blue shirt I got you, too. The one you've never worn."

I go to my room to read. It's something that I keep to myself. I know that none of my friends read, and I don't want to look different. It suddenly seems stupid to let other people's opinions matter so much. I always knew that I could've taken more advanced courses in school, that I'm smart enough. But I worried that I wouldn't fit in with my friends if I did too well. It had always been easier to act stupid. Now I realize what stupid really was.

I'm reading *Mercy Among the Children*. I'm lost in the story, when suddenly something occurs to me: What am I going to do for shoes? All I have are my old crappy ones, work boots, plus a beat-up pair of cross-trainers, now flecked with white paint.

I call a taxi and head to the mall, wishing Amber was here to help me pick something out. I end up buying a brown leather pair with laces and thick soles. I've seen other kids wearing the same shoes, but they always looked like they'd be uncomfortable.

As soon as I leave the mall, I take off my sneakers and put on the shoes, figuring that, if I walk home in them, they won't look so brand new later tonight. I gently scuff them against the curb a few times and drag my feet as I veer off the sidewalk into the weeds and shrubs. Of course, I end up stepping in dog shit.

It must've been a big dog, like a moose-dog, because it looks like I've stepped in a cow-pie. It's fresh enough to roll right up over both sides of the shoe. By the time I get home, I've gotten most of it scrapped off by dragging my foot and scraping it with a stick. Still, I have to scrub it in the bathroom sink with a scouring pad. Mom's not exactly impressed with the stink I've dragged through the house.

When Amber pulls up at seven-thirty, I'm waiting

in the yard, all pressed and dressed to kill. I climb into the car and we're off. I'm nervous, and sweating way too much, plus I can't stop taking long, deep breaths through my nose to see if there's any lingering odour of dog crap.

"You smell something?" Amber says.

Please, no, I think. Maybe I've gotten so used to it I can't smell it anymore.

"No, do you?" I ask, trying to sound casual.

"I thought you did, the way you were breathing," she says.

"Oh, that. That's just because you smell really great," I say, proud of my recovery.

***

We pull up in front of Amber's parents' house. I figure there's at least a million bucks' worth of vehicles parked around the place. Amber parks beside a sleek BMW, which is bumper-to-bumper with a Mercedes. A little further up, there's even a Hummer. That's what I call really flaunting it, because honestly, who needs a car that big?

"Ready?" Amber asks as we get out.

"Ready as I'll ever be," I say.

"We won't stay long, so just relax, okay? And try not to swallow your tongue when you meet Myrna, all right?" she says as she leads me through the ornate front door.

The house is full of well-dressed men and women. The smell of cologne and perfume is overpowering. Every time someone moves, jewellery flashes, and I can't help thinking Jordan would see this as the perfect takedown.

"Amber, sweetheart. Elias," her Mom gushes as she hurries over to us. "So glad you could make it." She seems surprised. The down-to-earth lady from the barbeque is nowhere to be found.

Everyone already knows Amber, but I get introduced around. All the men give me hearty, manly handshakes, while the women offer me their hands like I'm supposed to kiss them. I almost burst out laughing when I imagine holding one of them tightly by the fingers and then licking their knuckles. Weird what you'll think of when you're uncomfortable.

"This is Myrna," I hear Amber say. I turn to see a woman who looks like she stood too close to something really hot. Her face looks shrunken on her skull. Her expression is frozen into a look someone might have if you tossed a live weasel at them. Bad facelift, I decide.

"How do you do?" I say.

"Fine, thank you," she says. It was like someone in the crowd had thrown their voice. Her face is like wax; even her lips barely move. Then I notice the breasts.

They're huge, and sticking straight out from her chest. Unless she's wearing a cast-iron bra, it wasn't just her face that she'd had done over. Amber sees my expression, and I guess I haven't hidden my shock very well, because she bursts out laughing.

"Sorry, I just thought of something," she lies.

"Are those the same shoes?" Myrna asks.

"Pardon me?" I ask.

"Your shoes. Are they from two different pairs?" she says.

I look down at my feet. To my horror I see that the one I scoured is no longer brown. It's turned a reddish colour. I'd left them in the porch after I cleaned them. The light isn't so good in there, so I hadn't noticed when I'd put them on.

"I stepped in dog shit," I say.

Amber busts out laughing again, and Myrna flees to get her glass refilled. Then Amber's dad announces it's time to open the presents. Amber stands beside me as everyone fawns over the selection of gifts. It seems like her mom will never get to her present.

"Makes you almost wish for one of those alien abductions, doesn't it?" Amber whispers to me.

"Yeah, I could go for a good alien plucktion," I agree. Amber lets out a strange little squeal as she tries to stifle her laugh. "My money is on Myrna to be their leader."

Amber's gift is finally opened, and her Mom declares that it will go perfectly in the "Sitting Room." Where I live, they're all sitting rooms, unless they're "Laying Rooms." Anyway, the main thing is that we can leave now.

"So what'd you think?" Amber asks as we head for her car.

"You don't want to know," I say.

"What was it like to be around a bunch of people who all have a lot of money?" she asks.

I give her a look that lets her know how surprised I am by the question. She looks a little embarrassed, so I answer her.

"I couldn't care less how much money they have," I say as we get in. "They're just people with money. No big deal. As long as they're happy, I guess."

"Do you think money can make you happy?"

"You tell me," I say.

"All that perfume has given me a headache. Do you mind if I drop you home?" she says.

"Sure, whatever," I reply. I figure I must've said something to upset her, but I'm wrong. When we get to my place, she kisses me goodnight, and asks me if I'd like to see a movie the next weekend.

After the promise in that kiss, I quickly agree.

Chapter 12

I spend the next week at work thinking of two things: I'll get to see Amber again that weekend, and that I have to find the courage to tell Jordan that, as far as the takedown is concerned, I'm out.

Every attempt I make backfires on me. Whenever the topic comes up, he just gets excited about how much money we're going to get, and I lose my nerve. On Friday after work, the week before it's supposed to go down, Jordan drops in on his way over to Tanya's.

"I talked to The Chest again," he says, as we sit outside smoking.

"Yeah?" I say, hoping he'll tell me she changed her mind and the deal is off.

"She's still in," he says. "And she can get her mom's car anytime, so were on."

"Great," I say, letting another chance to walk away from the whole deal slip by. I wonder if maybe I'm just not really very brave.

I stay home for the evening, and around eight o'clock Amber calls. She'll pick me up the next evening at seven, and tells me she's excited. No more than I am, I think. I'm still finding it hard to believe that she's interested in me.

Saturday, I finish painting the house. There's no sign of Jordan, and I'm hoping that maybe he's changed his mind about the takedown. I finally get the nerve up to call him while I'm waiting for Amber to arrive, but he's not home. I tell his mother to have him call me, then sit on the step waiting. Amber pulls in right on time, and I try not to look too excited.

We're pulling out onto the street when she says, "I was thinking, since we've got lots of time before the movie starts, maybe we could stop by the pool hall."

"You don't want to go to the pool hall," I tell her. I figure she's just trying to show me she isn't too stuck-up to slum it a little.

"No, really, I do," she insists.

"Okay then," I say.

I smell the weed as soon as we get out of the car. There's a group of people on the sidewalk out front, passing around a joint and a bottle of cheap wine.

"Yo, Eli, good job with the stick," someone says as we get near.

"Right," I say, moving past them before Amber hears any more.

The place is full, and as we walk in the noise level drops. Half the people in there are looking at us like we just climbed out of a spaceship. The girls are staring at Amber in her designer clothes like they want to spit on her. I should have listened to my instincts. Bringing her here was a bad idea.

Jordan and Tanya are over by the video games. I steer Amber in their direction. Jordan's half-wasted, and throws his arms around Amber when I introduce her, almost taking both of them down when he loses his balance.

"Take it easy, Jordan," I tell him.

"It's okay," Amber says, but I've already seen the look on her face.

"Tanya, this is Amber," I say.

Amber smiles and says, "Hi, Tanya."

"Yeah," Tanya mutters.

"Hey, you want a shot of vodka?" Jordan asks.

"No thanks, we just dropped by before the movie," I say.

"You too good to drink with us?" he asks.

I don't answer, which is a mistake. Jordan doesn't like to be ignored.

"Hey, Amber, you should have seen this guy the other night," he says, with an evil glint in his eyes. "He had time for his friends then. Enough time that he nearly took a guy's head off with a pool cue."

"We've got to go," I say. "Come on, Amber."

"Nice meeting you, Tanya," Amber says.

"Yeah," Tanya replies.

"By the way, nice shirt, buddy," Jordan says with a smirk.

"Asshole," I mutter.

We're just turning to leave when Tina comes storming in. She walks straight over to Jordan, who looks like he wants to run.

"Who do you think you are?" she demands. "Do you think you can just use me, and then ignore me?"

He recovers his wits quickly, telling her to follow him outside. He's walking toward the door when he looks back to see if The Chest is following him. Right behind her is Tanya.

"No," Jordan says. "This is private, between me and Tina. I'll just be a minute."

Tanya is fuming as she turns back. I wonder how Jordan's going to weasel out of this one, and wish I could hang around for the fireworks. I look at Amber, who looks like she's about to panic, and decide against it.

"Ready?" I say.

Outside, we pass by Jordan and Tina just as she's threatening to go back inside and talk to Tanya. I don't feel sorry for him at all.

I walk around Amber's car to get in. The word "SLUT" is scratched into the paint on the passenger door. I'm instantly furious, but so ashamed that I don't even tell her. These are the people I grew up with. I've hung out with some of them my whole life, but right now I'm ashamed I even know them.

"Well, that was interesting," Amber says as we drive away.

"Sorry." I don't know what else to say.

"So, they don't like me?" she wants to know.

"I guess not."

"Because?" she asks.

"Because you're not one of them. Because you come from a different world. I don't know why," I say.

"But you're not like that?" she asks.

"Why should I be?" I ask her. "It's just jealousy, mainly. They think *you* think you're better than they are. None of them drove down there tonight in a new car their daddy bought them. It's like they think you're shoving what they don't have in their faces. So they have to find a way to turn it around. If they snub you first, you never get the chance to snub them, I guess. "

It suddenly occurs to me that I've explained myself to her too. "There's more to it, though," I add. "There's always stuff going on — someone with heavy shit to deal with. Like Tanya. She's pregnant. They just found out."

"Wow," she says. "She's like what, sixteen?"

"She just turned sixteen, actually."

"What's the story with Tina?"she asks.

"It's pretty obvious, isn't it?" I say.

"A lot of those girls get pregnant young, don't they?"

"What girls?" I ask. I don't like where this is headed.

91

"Girls from, you know, low-income families," she says.

"Yeah, you're right," I say. It's the truth.

"Then they drop out of school, go on welfare? Most of the time the father leaves, then the kids grow up and repeat the process," she states.

"Sounds like you got us all figured out," I say.

"I didn't mean you. You're different," she says. I wonder if that's true. Am I different than my friends?

"Let's drop it, okay?" I say.

"Okay," she says.

We're early for the movie, so after I buy our tickets, we play a video game. Big Game Safari. I let her win.

"I'm going to get some popcorn. You want some?" she asks.

"I'll get it," I say.

"No, you paid for the tickets, I'll pay for the snacks," she says.

I want to tell her that *she* isn't really paying for anything. Her parents are.

***

We're crossing the lobby when all hell breaks loose. There's a flood of girls coming from every direction, and it seems like every one of them is talking at once. A tall redhead sees us and rushes over. She gushes about how great it is to see Amber, asks how university is going, and squeals that they just have to get together soon. Amber introduces me, then tells them that we've just come from the pool hall.

"Amber, you're *so* ghetto," one of them teases.

She laughs, and we excuse ourselves and head off to the chick flick Amber has picked. She finds us seats way up near the back. Thankfully when her noisy friends show up, they don't see us.

The previews come on. It seems like the camera shots are in extreme close-up, and it's all way too loud. Our movie comes on, and Amber flips the arm between our seats up and snuggles up as close to me as she can get. I want to put my arm around her, but can't. I'm too worried that my deodorant might fail me. As I'd expected, the movie sucks.

It's a sappy love story with a bunch of dancing and singing, and all of it is too loud and in your face. After about an hour of this torture, I excuse myself to go to the washroom. Then I go outside for a smoke.

I'm leaning against the building, wondering how long I can stay away without ticking Amber off, when I notice the purple lights. The shitheads from the pool hall a couple of weeks ago have idled right up in front of me without my noticing them.

My guts tighten, and I wonder if I can make a run for it, or if I could live with myself if I did. There are six of them in the car. The guy Jordan stomped on is in the window next to me. He holds up his hand, encased in a cast, and smiles at me. I smile back and take a drag off my smoke. That's rule number one: Never show fear.

The car pulls away, but I get the message. They'll find me, or us, sometime, somewhere, without people around, and try to settle the score. It never ends. That's the reason for rule number two: Always watch your back.

I toss my butt and go back inside. The screen is still filled with dancing and singing. It finally ends and, as we funnel out with the crowd, Amber takes my hand, leaning into me.

"Did you enjoy it?" she asks.

"It was all right," I lie.

"You're a sweetie," she says.

The passenger side of Amber's car is facing us as we walk toward it. I brace myself for the moment when she sees the graffiti decorating it. If only she'd glanced back when we first arrived, I might have been spared from watching that movie.

We round the last row of cars and hers comes into view. She freezes instantly, dropping my hand as she stares in shock at her car. I wonder if she's trying to convince herself that it isn't really hers.

"Those pigs," she says. "Those filthy bitches."

"Who?" I ask.

"Those pieces of trash at the pool hall. Who do you think I mean?" she says.

"If this happened at the pool hall, don't you think I might've mentioned it?" I ask.

"Oh God, I'm sorry Elias," she says.

"Why?" I ask her. "Are you sorry because those are the people I hang out with? Because you assume that they're capable of doing something like this?"

"Don't be mean, Elias. I'm upset, that's all. Who could've done this? I just don't understand," she whines.

I don't want to play this game any longer, so I suggest she call the cops. She does, and I light a smoke while we wait for them to arrive.

At least it's not the same cops who took Jordan and me in who respond to the call. They ask a bunch of questions, including who might've had something against one of us. We both say we can't think of anyone. Of course, only one of us is telling the truth.

"So, Elias, you said you went out for a cigarette halfway through the movie, right?" one cop asks.

"Yes," I agree.

"But you didn't go near the car, correct?" he says.

"That's right," I say.

"You two been arguing, by any chance?" he asks. I'm just about to lose my temper when Amber speaks.

"Are you joking?" she asks him. "Elias?" She looks questioningly at me.

"Just doing my job, missy," the cop says.

"Amber," she says. "My name's Amber."

The cop takes a few notes and then tells Amber to report the vandalism to her insurance company. The whole time, Amber refuses to look at me. The cops say they'll stay on top of it, whatever that's supposed to mean, then they leave.

Amber is quiet as she drives me home. I wrack my brain for something to say to undo the night we've just had.

"So, what are you taking in college?" I ask.

"*Majoring* in," she says. "And it's university."

"Okay, what are you *majoring* in at *university*?" I ask.

"Sociology," she says sharply.

I get the picture and stop trying to make conversation. If it was my car, I'd be pissed off too.

When she gets to my place, instead of pulling into my yard she stops on the street out front.

"Well, other than my car getting vandalized, it was a fun evening," she says.

"Yeah, well, don't forget your warm welcome at the pool hall," I remind her.

"People are who they are," she says. "I guess I'll see you around. Maybe I'll give you a call."

"Don't bother," I say as I get out. I'm pretty sure that's the end of Amber's low-rent dating. Call it a sociology experiment gone wrong.

Chapter 13

On Sunday morning I'm wandering around the yard collecting cigarette butts when I hear a car pull up out front. I'm surprised to find myself excited at the thought that it might be Amber.

It's not. It's an old woman with a flat tire. As I come around the house to investigate, she's getting out of her car, and when she sees me, she breaks into a huge smile. I smile back.

"Good morning," she says, as if a flat tire isn't worth being unhappy about. I like her.

"How are you?" I ask.

"I'm just fine," she says. "How are you?"

"Good," I say. "Do you have a spare?"

"I believe there's one in the trunk. I can call someone, though," she says.

"Not a problem, ma'am," I reply. "Could you pop the trunk?"

I've never changed a tire before, but it's pretty

straightforward. Well, except for trying to figure out how the jack operates. As I work, she rambles on about her family, and how proud she is of her grandchildren. I find it hard not to laugh, but I figure maybe she's just a little nervous.

"I'm Iris, by the way," she says as I'm replacing the hubcap.

"Elias," I say. "Pleased to meet you."

I think I've said something wrong, or even worse, maybe she's the grandmother of someone I've kicked the shit out of. I'm the only Elias that I know of in Helmsdale.

"Are you all right?" I ask as her mouth drops open and her eyes go slightly out of focus. Then I think maybe she's having a stroke. Mr. Daniels from up the street had one, and his face is all twisted into a permanent sneer. I duck him now, because I can't make out what he's saying anymore.

"Yes, I'm fine," she says. "Goodness, I love coincidence. The pastor spoke just this morning on prophets. Elias in particular. Isn't that strange?"

"I guess," I say.

"So, do *you* see the future, Elias?" she says as she retrieves her purse from the car.

"Yes ma'am," I say. "I see me *not* taking a penny from you for the tire change."

"Are you sure?" she says.

"Yes," I reply. I've actually enjoyed her company.

She pulls away, and I sit on the step in the warm sunshine. I think about what it would be like if I could see into my future, if I knew exactly how things would turn out. I come to the conclusion that life would be pretty boring without any surprises at all.

Changing that tire gets me to thinking about Mr. Tarver, and what I did to him. For the first time in my life, I don't try to justify what I've done when the guilt hits. Instead, I think about what it would be like if I was him. Was he nervous now, unable to relax in his own home? Did he walk outside every morning expecting the worst?

I look up to see Jordan walking into my yard. His eyes are bloodshot and, as he gets close, I can smell stale booze on his breath.

"What's up?" he says.

"Nothing. I was just thinking about Tarver," I say. "Maybe we should've waited until we knew for sure what he was doing at the police station. He could've been there for any reason, you know?"

"He's an idiot. Besides, I had nothing to do with it. You were the one who got all wired and went after him. Give me a smoke," he says.

"What do you mean?" I say, as I hand him a cigarette. "We decided together, right?"

"No, I just agreed with you. Anyway, there's nothing you can do about it now," he says.

I don't remember exactly how it went down, but I'm pretty sure I'm not the only one to blame for it.

"What's the story on Tina?" I ask. "She was pretty freaked out at the pool hall, is she still in?" If she's not, I'll have found my way out of the takedown.

"Oh yeah, she's fine, everything's cool," he

says. "That was something else."

"I know. I saw you guys the morning after Butch's party. How did you explain it all to Tanya?"

"Don't worry about it," he says. "This time next week we'll be counting our money. I got to get home and catch some sleep, I feel like crap. I'll see you in the morning."

He's walking away when I say, "That decision to slash Tarver's tires was both of us." I can't get it through my mind that I'd do something like that on my own.

"Whatever," he says, flicking his butt onto the lawn.

I go inside to read, but I can't concentrate. I fix myself a sandwich for lunch, then check out my money situation. There's three hundred and sixty dollars tucked away in my sock drawer, and I pocket three hundred of it and go for a walk.

I wander around downtown, then follow the old train line along the river. Last year they took up the tracks, a pretty good sign that Helmsdale is down, and not getting back up anytime soon. I cut through the woods up to town and, before I know it, I'm passing by Tarver's place.

His car is gone, so I circle around and slip into his yard through the same hedge I used as cover on my last visit. I drop three hundred dollars into his mailbox. I hope it's enough money, and wish that I had the balls to face him. I'm starting to see myself clearly, and I'm not too happy with what I'm looking at.

I'm just leaving the step when the door opens behind me, and I freeze in my tracks. I wonder if I can get away with just telling him that I dropped by to ask about keeping up my school work from home.

"Elias?" he says.

I turn around to face him just as he's looking at the mailbox. He reaches for it, and I think that he must've heard me open it somehow, and that he's going to look inside. I hold my breath as he reaches out and pushes the flap down snugly.

"I was just wandering around, thought I'd drop in and say hello," I tell him.

"You should've knocked," he says.

"I saw your car wasn't home," I say.

"I lent it to a neighbour," he explains. "I just made coffee. Care for some?"

I have no choice. I tell him black is fine, and he goes inside to pour. I want to grab my money and run now, but I can see him through the screen door.

"Come on around back," he says, handing me the coffee. I follow him into the backyard and take a seat across from him at the picnic table. I take a sip as he smiles pleasantly at me, as if he really thinks I've made a friendly visit.

"So, what's new?" he asks.

"I'm working, me and Jordan, for his uncle," I say. "Carpentry work. Well, mostly labour, but I like it."

"That's good," he says. "Are you thinking of becoming a carpenter?"

"It was me," I say before I even realize what I'm doing. He tilts his head and looks at me, wondering what I'm talking about.

"The tires," I say. "I slashed your tires. We, I mean *I,* thought you ratted us out, you know, at the cop station, the day of the fight. I'm sorry."

"I used to be like you," he says. He doesn't say any more, and I stare at my coffee, waiting. It gets uncomfortable quickly, so I have to say something.

"How's that?" I ask.

"I guess I thought the world was against me," he says. "One day I figured it out, and realized I was against the world. There's a big difference. It took a lot of courage to come here, Elias. A lot more courage than your last trip."

"Thank you for the coffee," I say, downing the rest of it. I just want to be gone.

"Anytime," he says. "I hope to see you in class again."

As I walk home, I wonder what Jordan would think of what I've just done. I know he would never admit that he was wrong, and that apologizing would be considered a sign of weakness. Maybe I'll tell him what I did, just so he knows that I'm my own man.

Chapter 14

Hank picks me up Monday morning and we drive over to Jordan's place. His mom comes out to tell us that he's not feeling well, and that he won't be working today. I figure he's probably just hung over.

"You guys partying last night?" Hank says as we drive away.

"I wasn't," I reply.

"I need guys I can depend on. You know anything about that generator?"

"The Honda?" I ask.

"Yeah. I tied it on the truck myself, but when Rob got to the shop, it was gone. Supposedly it fell off the truck, but I knew it didn't. I thought it over and went back to Keating's place, and I found where it had been sitting in the bushes, out by the street. I could see the grass all flattened, and a spot of oil where the crank is leaking."

"Maybe it fell off there?" I say. Is he asking me if I know anything about it, because he suspects I'm involved?

"No, it was five feet from the driveway. I would've seen where it rolled if it had fallen off," he says with a sigh.

"I had nothing to do with it, Hank," I tell him. I'm scared that, if he thinks I was in on it, he'll fire me.

"I know that, Eli," he says.

We stop at the hardware store, where he pays eleven hundred dollars for a new generator. I think that, if Jordan stole the old one, he was lucky if he got two hundred for it. Hank drops me off at a house, where I spend the day ripping out water-soaked drywall from a basement that flooded. Its filthy work, and it stinks. By lunchtime I'm exhausted.

I arrive home after work to find Mom passed out on the couch, and I pour her booze down the sink and sit the bottle back on the floor beside her. I make myself a sandwich for supper, smoke a joint, and sit on the step daydreaming about a different life. I don't see Jordan until he's right in front of me.

"How was work?" he says with a smirk.

"Good," I say. "Where were you?"

"I had better things to do," he says.

"Like what?"

"Hey, anything's better than wet drywall," he says. Now I'm pissed off. I worked alone in that crap all day because he didn't want to.

"What happened to the generator?" I ask.

"What makes you think I'd know anything about it?" he demands. "Hank tied it on. Maybe he should be more careful."

Unless Jordan had been talking to someone from work over the weekend, he wouldn't know what I had meant.

"You talking to anyone since Friday evening, from work?" I ask.

"No, why?" he says.

"Just wondering," I say.

"Strange question," he says, and I can picture the gears turning in his head.

"You working tomorrow?" I ask.

"Yeah, I guess. Did you finish where you were?"

"Almost," I say. I'm lying. There's another full day for both of us left.

"Let's head down to Sam's. I've got some killer weed," he says. "It's that Afghan Skunk crossbreed shit."

"I'm pretty tired. You got much? I wouldn't mind a little hit for later," I say.

He pulls out a bag, most of an ounce, and hands me a good-sized bud. It goes for four hundred dollars an ounce.

I roll up a small joint after he leaves, and I'm right in the middle of breathing my way through an anxiety attack, when a taxi pulls into the yard. I'm so messed up that, even though I want to send it away, I can only concentrate on my breathing.

Mom comes out and pays the driver for the

bottle, then walks back in by me without saying a word. I know she can smell the weed. They don't call it Skunk for nothing.

When I finally get myself together, I go inside and pack a lunch for work the next day. Mom's watching TV, and we ignore each other as I walk by her on my way to my room. It's not worth the hassle to mention her drinking. I'm not going to be around that long anyway. Even if I go to jail for the assault rap, I'm pretty sure they'll have some sort of school there. When I graduate, I'm out of Helmsdale for good.

I lie on the bed thinking about the takedown, jail, Amber, Mom drinking, and on and on until the munchies overtake me. I head to the kitchen and gorge myself on crackers and peanut butter, then go outside for one last smoke before bed.

I'm standing out behind the house, next to the woods that borders our backyard, when I happen to glance back and see a car cruising slowly down our street. I can see the purple lights around the windshield, and, as it passes under a streetlight, I see that it's the guys from the pool hall again. There's four or five of them in the car, and I wonder what I'll do if they land looking for trouble.

I light another smoke and walk over to the house, leaning against it in the dark. I wish I had a gun, and think maybe I'll check with Jordan about getting one. Not that I'd shoot anyone. I figure that just the act of pulling one out would do the trick.

I'm just finishing my smoke, when I see some-one moving along the bushes on the upper side of our yard. They must've come from the street, and there's no reason for them to be there. It's dark, but I can see enough from the streetlights to tell me that whoever it is has a bottle in their hand. I watch them disappear behind our shed, at the back of the yard.

With my heart hammering against my ribs, I hustle quietly down the other side of the shed. I take a cautious peek around the corner, but there's no one there. I hope that whoever it is has gone into the woods, and keeps on going. I move to the far corner and take another peek up the side of the shed, and there he is, silhouetted in the streetlight.

It takes me only a second to register what I see, just about the same time as I smell the gasoline. He's pouring it over the side of the building, and he never hears me coming. My fist crashes into his side, from behind, and he grunts as he col-lapses to the ground. He lies there wheezing as I pick up the pop bottle and pour the last bit of gas onto his head.

The fear must give him strength, because he manages to roll over and start to crawl as I pull out my lighter. I stomp down between his shoulders, pinning him to the ground with my foot. Leaning over, I hold the lighter close to the side of his face and spark it. It's the guy from the pool hall, the one with the goatee.

"Please," he groans.

"Shh, I'm thinking," I say. He lies there helplessly as I think it over. If I let him go, will they be back? Do I want to live with the fact that I've actually set fire to someone? If I do, where will it end, since then they'll really have a reason to seek revenge? All I know for sure is that I'm sick of this life.

"Go," I say, straightening up and stepping back from him. He slowly stands up and starts to hobble away.

"The bottle," I say.

He comes back and gets it, keeping his face down so he doesn't have to look at me. I walk out to the street behind him, but there's no sign of the car. He limps off around the corner, and I go back in the house. Suddenly I'm exhausted, and I don't stir until the alarm clock buzzes me awake.

Chapter 15

Jordan's waiting when we pull into his yard the next morning, and when we get to work, he sees how much is left to be done. He stays in a pissy mood all day, which I actually enjoy.

There's no mention of the takedown until Jordan brings it up Friday afternoon. I'm ready for him. I made my mind up after the incident at my house on Sunday night.

"You ready for Sunday morning?" he says as we're packing up our tools.

"Yeah," I say.

"You excited?" he asks.

"I guess," I tell him. "This is it, then I'm done."

"As long as I can count on you," he says.

I'm a nervous wreck all day Saturday, wandering around the house and yard until I'm dizzy. I go to Sniper Sam's to kill some time that evening, but suddenly I can't take everyone's bullshit anymore, and wander back home.

I barely sleep Saturday night, finally giving up and getting out of bed at two-thirty. I'm out in the yard, jacked on coffee and cigarettes and lack of sleep, when Jordan shows up right on time at five o'clock.

One more quick rundown on the details, and we head off in the early morning light. We keep to the back streets and alleyways, and we're hiding in the bushes outside the motel by a quarter to six. My heart is beating wildly, and the coffee is burning my guts.

Jordan pulls a black ski mask out of his pocket and hands it to me. I hope he doesn't notice my hands trembling. I just want this over with. I don't even care about the money anymore.

"There he is," he suddenly hisses. I peek out to see Jack Hargrove pulling up to the door of room number six. He gets out of his car with a bag in his hand. He knocks, and I'm glad to see how old and small the guy is who opens the door. Suddenly I've got to piss so bad that I'm shivering.

I move off a way and relieve myself, and I'm barely back when Jack comes out of the room and drives off. Jordan has brought a watch, and he pulls it out to check the time.

"Perfect," he says. "Now, if that stupid bitch can tell time, we've got it made."

We wait a few more minutes, then he nods toward the room and moves off. I circle around through the bushes and come up beside the motel, right around the corner from room six. My mind is blank as I try not to hyperventilate. I haven't put my mask on yet. I figure, if someone happens along, I can just pretend I'm out for a walk.

A long time seems to pass, then suddenly someone grabs my arm from behind. I barely stifle a yell as I turn to face Jordan.

"Calm down," he whispers. "Tina's late. Five more minutes and I'm going in myself."

"Wait," I say, as he turns to leave. "You can't just knock on the door. He'll see you through the peephole. You think he's going to open the door for a guy in a mask?"

"I'll put my finger over it. Do I have to think of everything?" he says.

"He won't open it if he can't see who's there," I say. "Let's drop it. We'll figure out something else and come back next week."

"I'll kick it open if I have to," he says. He heads back to his position.

Minutes later I hear a car. I glance around the corner to see Tina pull up in front of room four and shut off her car. She sits there, looking puzzled, and I have no choice but to risk stepping out of my position. I catch her attention with a wave, as she smiles and waves back. I hold up six fingers, then point to the room. I hear the car pulling forward, followed by a long blare from the horn.

I peek around the corner, and she's standing there facing the room. She looks at me and says, "Where's shithead?"

"Turn around," I hiss.

She turns around just as the motel room door opens and I hear a voice say, "Having trouble, darling?"

I take a deep breath and duck back down behind the corner. The old guy is walking toward Tina when I nail him from the side in a bear-hug. I lift him up and spin toward the room, just as the door clicks shut. I hope he doesn't start yelling.

Jordan races up and grabs the doorknob, but it's locked. He takes a quick scan of our captive and snatches a room key that's dangling from his shirt pocket. Looking at Jordan, I realize that I forgot to put my mask on.

Jordan tries to shove the key in the lock but drops it. As he bends to retrieve it, the old guy takes a casual kick at his head. His shoe bounces off Jordan's forehead. Not hard, but more like a reward for being so stupid. It leaves a mark, but Jordan's so intent on getting us inside he doesn't even seem to notice.

"You guys are screwed," he says when Jordan finally gets the door open.

I hustle the old guy inside. Suddenly I don't know what to do with him, so I just stand there with my arms wrapped around him. Jordan yells "Go!" at Tina as he's shutting the door, and she yells back at him, "To hell with you, Jordan Black!"

I groan when I hear her use his full name. Maybe she's not so stupid after all.

"Where's the money?" Jordan demands.

"What money?" the old guy says.

"The goddamned gambling-machine money!" Jordan shouts as he pulls a handgun from the waistband of his pants. He makes a big show of cocking it, and I let go of my hostage. I step over next to Jordan, who's pointing the gun right at the old guy's head.

"Easy, it's right here. Put that gun down," he says, walking over to the table beside the bed. There's a satchel, like a big purse, sitting there. His back is to us as he picks it up, and I think he's opening it to show us the money. He spins around with a smile, levelling a vicious looking 9mm Automatic at Jordan's face.

"Drop it!" he bellows. Jordan has lowered his gun so that it's dangling in his hand, down by his thigh. He sees that it's over, and tosses his weapon out in front of us onto the floor.

There's a split second when I hope the old guy isn't going to kill us. Then there's a sharp cracking sound, and I feel a tug at my side. I look down to see a neat hole through my jacket pocket, a thin trail of blood running from it. I'm strangely relieved when I realize the shot came from Jordan's gun.

I put my hand over the hole and tell them, "I'm hit." Jordan is slack-jawed and white as a sheet. The old guy grabs his bag and hurries for the door. I slowly squat down to the floor, then roll onto my side. Now my stomach feels like it's on fire. I hear the door open and close, then

Jordan says my name.

"Shit," I say.

"You're okay. You'll be all right," he says as he kneels beside me, tucking his gun into his pocket. "It didn't go through."

I don't understand why it's good that the bullet is still inside me. "Call 911," I say.

"Wait, not from here. We've got to move," he says. He pulls me to my feet and throws my arm over his shoulder. He wraps one of his around my waist. He walks me to the door, pulls it open with his free hand, and pushes me through in front of him. He catches me as I start to topple over. If I could, I'd yell for help. He gets me to the dumpster near the corner of the parking lot, sitting me down with my back leaning against it.

"You okay?" he asks.

"I'm shot, man." I manage to gasp. "Get me help." Exhaustion washes over me, and, for some reason, my feet are cold. I tilt my head back to look up at him, and he grimaces like he's the one that has a bullet in his guts.

"I'm sorry, Elias," he says as he turns and sprints away. I haven't got the strength to tell him he's headed in the wrong direction. All I want now is to sleep.

Chapter 16

When I open my eyes again, I see a blurry ceiling.
I try to swallow, but can't. I let my eyes fall shut.
As I drift back to the safe dark place where I'd
been, I think I hear a name spoken. *Elias.* But it
means nothing to me.

I smell apples and, when I open my eyes again,
there's a face close to mine. A pretty face, with
bright blue eyes. I try to smile. She smiles back,
and I think I'd like to kiss that face.

"Hi, I'm Melinda," she says softly. "I'm a student nurse. You're in the hospital, and everything
is fine. We're glad you're back with us."

I don't remember being with them before, and I
really need a drink. I try to tell her that, but I can't
talk because my throat is so dry. It feels like there's
something stuck in there. Melinda leans over me to
check something on a monitor. I discover that it's
her hair that smells like apples.

"Don't try to talk, okay?" she says. "Stay calm. I'll get the nurse in charge. You'll be fine."

I like Melinda. With Melinda, everything is fine.

I close my eyes, and a memory pops into my mind. I remember taking what I think is my last breath, and the smell of garbage. Oddly, I don't recall any fear.

"Elias?" a voice says. "I'm Dr. Linton. You've had a bit of a trauma, but everything is under control. Can you hear me?"

"Yes," I squawk. "Water."

"We'll get that tube out right away. How do you feel?"

"Thirsty," I say.

"Do you remember what happened?" he asks. I make a quick decision and shake my head no.

"You were the victim of an assault. You've suffered a gunshot wound to your abdomen. Your liver was damaged, just a small nick, but you lost a lot of blood. That was on Sunday. This is Wednesday."

"My mother?" I say.

"Somebody is calling her right now. I assume she'll be here shortly. We have to contact the police, they'll need some information. In the meantime, let's get that breathing tube out."

I've still got an IV and a catheter in me, but at least they give me an ice-cube to suck on. I never knew how great it was to be able to swallow.

Mom shows up, and I smell booze mixed with mouthwash. I'm sure she must've been through a lot while I was out. So it's okay.

"What happened, Eli?" she sobs.

"I don't remember," I lie.

She doesn't say anything else for a long time, then, with a big sigh, she says, "I can't lose you, Elias."

"Go home, Mom, and get some rest. I'll be all right. Things will be different now."

"Yes," she replies.

After she leaves, I run the whole situation through my head again. I remember Jordan running for help, and realize that my life had been in his hands. If he hadn't made that call, Mom would be all alone. I wonder how long it would have taken her to drink herself to death.

They give me another needle, and I slip back into peaceful darkness. By morning I'm feeling fully alert, and if I don't move, nothing hurts. They give me something that resembles sand mixed with motor oil to drink, and call it breakfast. They tell me it's important that I drink it, so I do. I want Melinda to be pleased with me.

"Elias Minto?" I hear a voice say. I turn my head to see a cop in uniform, accompanied by a guy in a suit, standing in my doorway.

"Yes," I say.

"I'm Detective Barnes, this is Sergeant Thayer," the guy in the suit says. "We'd like to speak with you."

"Sure, come on in," I say. I want to get this part over and behind me.

"How are you feeling?" Barnes asks.

"Good, I guess," I tell him.

"You're a lucky man," he states, pulling a notebook from his pocket.

"I know," I say.

"So, tell us what you remember," he says.

"I couldn't sleep, so I went for a walk," I begin.

"What time was this?" he interrupts.

"Maybe six or so," I say. "I was down by the Bateman Motel. I was cutting across the parking lot, heading back home. I heard some guy ask me for a light. I turned around and he shot me. That's it."

"What was he wearing?" Barnes asks.

"I don't remember," I say.

"Did you see his face?"

"No, he had a ball cap on. He kept his face down, and the peak of the cap hid him," I say. He makes a note and exchanges a glance with the cop in uniform.

"What about his voice? Anything distinguishing about it? What did he say, exactly?"

"Hey, you got a light?" I say. "Then he shot me."

"Accent?"

"No," I say.

"Are you sure?" he says.

"Yeah, positive," I say. "Why is that so important?"

Just then someone out in the hall drops something. The sound of metal hitting the floor causes both cops to flinch. Me too, but I'm the only one who groans. It feels like my stomach ripped open.

"You need a nurse?" the cop in uniform asks.

"No," I say as the pain begins to recede.

"Okay, so you never saw his face, you recall no accent of any kind, and you don't remember what he was wearing. Is that correct so far, Elias?" Barnes says.

"Yeah," I say.

"Was he short or tall?" he says. I pick short.

"How short?"

"Pretty short," I say.

"Up to your knee?" Barnes says. It's not funny.

"What?" I say.

"Why don't you cut the bullshit, son," he says. "The bullet entered your body at a roughly forty-five-degree angle. Either this guy was lying down when the gun was fired, or you were."

He fixes me with a flat stare, waiting for me to admit I was lying. I've been through this before, and I know enough not to change my story. I reach up and press the buzzer pinned to my pillow. Like magic, Melinda appears. I'm smiling before I catch myself.

"What is it, Elias?" she asks.

"I need something for pain, my stomach really hurts," I say. What I really want is to be rid of the cops. Of course, the free buzz will be a bonus.

"We'll talk again," Barnes says. "Try to get things straight, all right? If you're protecting someone, well, don't be stupid."

The next day I move from Intensive Care to a

ward room. Jordan still hasn't been in to visit me. I figure he's feeling too guilty. After supper, I'm reading a four-month-old *Maclean's* magazine, when I hear a scuffing noise from the hall. It gets closer, and I realize what it is. Mr. Tarver walks into my room.

"Hello, Elias," he says with a grin. "How are you feeling?"

"All right, I guess," I say.

"I heard about what happened," he says. "I used to be like you. I've watched a lot of people flush their lives away. One day I found myself right where you are, lying in a hospital bed, ready to make a decision. That's where the cowlick comes from."

He stops, but I want to hear the rest. I've been in the hospital all week, and other than the cops and Mom, he's the only person who's come to visit me.

"I don't understand," I say.

"It was the same story: booze, drugs, fighting, just being what I thought was a tough guy. One night I got nailed in the back of the head with a wheel-wrench. My skull fractured, and I spent four months recovering. I've got a plate in there. It was decision time for me then. Same as it is for you now."

"Yeah, I've got that under control," I tell him.

"Good," he says, rising from the visitor's chair. "I've got to go. I also want to tell you that coming to my house is the bravest thing you've ever done. Not many men can admit when they've been wrong. I think you know it's time for a change, so I'm going to talk to my brother. He's a lawyer, and he can get you a deal. This is your chance. Use it wisely."

"I will," I say.

Mr. Tarver is just out the door when the detective returns. We go through the same routine, the same questions, with the same results. He's disgusted, because he knows I'm lying. There's nothing he can do. There's one thing about his questions that bothers me.

"By the way," I say to him as he's leaving. "Why is the shooter's voice so important? Do you have a suspect?"

"Not really," he says. "It's just that we thought it might be a possibility that the 911 call could have been made by the shooter. The guy who called it in had a French accent. That's all."

Epilogue

Six months later and I'm finally back home to stay. I've figured out a lot of things since that day Jordan and I were arrested, most of them good, some of them bad.

After three weeks in the hospital, I was well enough to go home, but not back to work. Getting a bullet fired into your guts doesn't cancel out any previous shit you've been involved in. So, shortly after getting out, I went to court for sentencing. I pled guilty, even though I still think I wasn't, because Mr. Tarver's brother the lawyer said it was the best idea.

I got three months in a shit-hole group home. The staff were all lazy, and stupid, and had no interest in being bothered with us. Except for the director, who was a cool older lady who could psyche you out with a glance. One day I was high, and she asked me if I was. She gave me that look and I had to say yes. Then she took me in her office so I could explain *why* I was high. But when I got there, I couldn't. That really got me thinking.

Mr. Tarver said that confessing to him was the bravest thing I'd ever done. It probably was, until I found the courage to ask Melinda out. With her in college, and being older than me, I figured it was a stretch. Plus, she probably wasn't involved in many situations where you could actually catch a bullet, or wanted to be.

She's my girlfriend now. Maybe more like a really good friend, who's also a girl. It's the first time I've ever had anyone to *really* talk to. She's smart, and funny. She makes me see things in myself that I overlooked before. She even convinced me to enrol in the classes I'll need if I ever want to go to college.

Mom still has a hard time with the booze. Instead of ignoring her, now I try to help her. I think she can turn things around, but that's her decision. Now, when she gets drunk, I don't run to Jordan's place.

There is no Jordan's place to run to.

I was out of the hospital for a week before he finally came to visit me. It was awkward. What do you say to a guy who left you for dead? I didn't let him know that I knew he abandoned me. It's all in the past, and our friendship was over anyway.

I did ask him where he'd made the 911 call from, just to see his reaction. For a few seconds, I thought I'd been wrong about the whole thing. He told me he'd flagged down a car, and got the driver to make the call from her cellphone. He said the lady was really nice.

Jordan never made it to court. The judge issued a warrant for his arrest, but they haven't found him yet. If the police can't find him, he's got to be completely off the radar. I heard from one of the Darwin brothers that Tanya aborted the baby in the end. Sometimes I think of Jordan, on the run from himself, and I always wish him well. Everyone has a choice.

Acknowledgements

I'm very grateful to my wife, Valerie, for all her support and love.

Thanks to my editor, Carrie Gleason, for all her work and patience. And thanks to my Posse, who are always inspiring. Life is good.

Read more great teen fiction from SideStreets.

Ask for them at your local library, bookstore, or order them online at www.lorimer.ca.

Wasted

by Brent R. Sherrard

Jacob likes to party, but, unlike his alcoholic father, he knows that he can easily overcome his drug and alcohol abuse. When when a terrible tragedy takes Jacob to the breaking point, he discovers just how powerful dependency can be.

ISBN: 978-1-55277-419-9 (paperback)

Out

by Sandra Diersch

No one in Alex's world is who they seem to be. Alex struggles with his faith when he witnesses a church member cheating on his wife and learns that his brother is gay. When his brother is brutally attacked, Alex is forced to decide where his loyalties lay and what he really believes in.

ISBN: 978-1-55277-421-2 (paperback)

New Blood

by Peter McPhee

After a gang of thugs beat him up, Callum's parents decide to move. But the problems don't end for Callum in their new town. Callum's deep inner scars make school a continuous battleground.

ISBN: 978-1-55028-996-1 (paperback)

LORIMER

Scab
by Robert Rayner

Julian Faye, aka Scab, knows all about being picked on. For years he's been bullied by his classmates and neglected by his parents. Now, seventeen and a gifted photographer, he's faced with a dilemma: Get the shot that'll launch his career, or save the only person who's ever given a damn about him.
ISBN: 978-1-55277-482-3 (paperback)

War Games
by Jacqueline Guest

Ryan's father is on his first tour of duty in Afghanistan, and Ryan is thrilled. He'll finally get a break from his overbearing father and be able to spend more time off the military base. But Ryan soon becomes entangled in a world of deceit, which forces him to come to terms with the extreme risks his father is facing overseas.
ISBN: 978-1-55277-035-1 (paperback)

All In
by Monique Polak

Todd's never been much of a student, but he's got plenty of street smarts and he's a mean poker player. Todd's always had a thing for Claire, the most beautiful girl in school, but Claire likes nice things. If Todd wants to date her, he'll need cash, and plenty of it. Soon, a weekly poker game turns into a costly and dangerous obsession, and Todd's luck begins to change.
ISBN: 978-1-55028-912-1 (paperback)